Luis forced her to look up at him

"Do not make my cousin Ramon fall in love with you. I should not find it amusing," he warned.

"I don't find any of this amusing," Nicola snapped. "But you don't have to worry. With an unwanted bridegroom in my life, I'm not likely to start encouraging anyone else!" She turned to leave, but he gripped her arm, pulling her around to face him.

"So, you don't want me," he said softly. "What a little hypocrite you are, *amiga*."

He bent his head and found her lips with his. His mouth moved slowly and persuasively, coaxing her lips apart in a sensually teasing caress that sent her blood hammering through her veins. All her resolutions about remaining aloof swiftly died as he drew her closer, his own urgency firing a response she was helpless to control.

SARA CRAVEN
is also the author of these

Harlequin Presents

and this

Harlequin Romance

Many of these books are available at your local bookseller.

For a free catalog listing all titles currently available,
send your name and address to:

HARLEQUIN READER SERVICE
1440 South Priest Drive, Tempe, AZ 85281
Canadian address: Stratford, Ontario N5A 6W2

SARA CRAVEN

counterfeit bride

Harlequin Books

TORONTO • NEW YORK • LOS ANGELES • LONDON
AMSTERDAM • PARIS • SYDNEY • HAMBURG
STOCKHOLM • ATHENS • TOKYO • MILAN

Harlequin Presents first edition January 1983
ISBN 0-373-10561-4

Original hardcover edition published in 1982
by Mills & Boon Limited

CHAPTER ONE

'You know something?' Elaine Fairmont announced. 'I'm really going to miss Mexico.'

Nicola looked up from the files she was packing into a carton, her lips curving in amusement.

'What's prompted this sudden, if belated, change of heart?' she enquired. 'I thought nothing in Mexico City could possibly compare with Los Angeles?'

'Well, I've been giving the matter some thought, and I've decided that actually they have quite a lot in common,' Elaine said solemnly. She began to count off on her fingers. 'There's the traffic and the smog—and the possibility of earthquakes—we mustn't forget those. Of course L.A. isn't actually sinking into a lake as far as I know, but the San Andreas fault could change all that.'

'It could indeed,' Nicola agreed, her eyes dancing. 'I suppose there's no chance that you'll change your mind a step further and come with me on my sightseeing trip?'

Elaine shook her head. 'No, honey. To me a ruin is a ruin, and who needs them? I'm no tourist, and besides, I've read about those Aztecs, and they had some pretty creepy habits. I'm not going back to L.A. with nightmares.' She paused. 'I suppose you haven't changed your mind either?'

'About returning to California with Trans-Chem?' It was Nicola's turn to shake her head. 'No, I've thoroughly enjoyed working for them, but this contract was really just a means to an end—a way of letting me see Mexico.' And a way of getting me as far away from Zurich and from Ewan as possible, she thought with a pang.

'So, sign another contract and see the U.S.A.,' Elaine

5

suggested amiably. 'Martin's all set to fix you up with a work permit the moment you say the word, and all my folks are dying to meet you.'

Nicola smiled. 'It's very tempting, I admit. But I'm not sure where I want to work next time. I think it will almost certainly be Europe again.'

'Then why not Spain?' Elaine asked. 'Your Spanish is terrific, thanks to Teresita's coaching. It would be a great chance to make use of it.'

'Perhaps.' Nicola gave a slight grimace. 'Actually I'd planned on finding somewhere a little more liberated next time.'

Elaine laughed. 'Don't tell me you've gotten tired of all this *guera preciosa* as you walk down the street?'

'I hate it.' There was a sudden intensity in Nicola's tone which made Elaine glance curiously at her before she returned to her task of feeding unwanted documents into the shredder. 'It's insulting. I haven't any illusions about my attractions, such as they are, and I don't need my ego boosted by meaningless compliments from total strangers. "Precious light-haired one" indeed! It's not even a particularly valid description,' she added, tugging at a strand of her tawny sun-streaked hair. 'Surely you of all people can't go along with this incessant reduction of women to mere sex objects?'

Elaine lifted a negligent shoulder. 'It doesn't really bother me. It's harmless as long as you don't take it seriously, or respond in any way, and I quite like being admired. The Women's Lib movement isn't the whole answer, you know. I've seen what it's done to people—to my own sister, in fact. She was happily married, or she sure seemed to be until someone started raising her consciousness. Now she's divorced, the kids cry all the time, and there's endless hassle with lawyers about alimony, and who gets the car and the ice-box.'

Nicola closed the carton and fastened it with sealing tape.

'That's rather going to extremes,' she said. 'What I

can't get used to is the attitude here that a woman is just—an adjunct to a man. Industrially, Mexico is making giant strides, but there are some things still which haven't changed from the days of the conquistadores—and that's what I find so hard to take. Well, look at Teresita, for instance.'

'I'm looking,' Elaine agreed. 'What's her problem?'

'Everything.' Nicola spread her hands helplessly. 'There's this guardian of hers. She's been sharing our apartment for three months now, and she still hasn't told him. He thinks she's living in that convent hostel, and from things she's said, I gather even that was a concession.'

Nicola's tone became heated, and Elaine smiled.

'Calm down,' she advised. 'If there was ever anyone who doesn't need our sympathy, then it's Teresita.'

'You mean because she's actually going to escape from the trap?' Nicola reached for another carton. 'I suppose you're right.'

'No, that wasn't what I meant,' Elaine said drily. 'Nor am I too sure she is going to escape, as you put it.'

Nicola put down the files she was holding, and stared at the other girl with growing concern.

'But of course she will, when she marries Cliff. He won't keep her chained up. Or are you saying you don't think they will get married?' When Elaine nodded, she burst out, 'But that's ridiculous! You've said yourself you've never seen two people so much in love. Why, she's living for him to get back from Chicago, you know she is.'

'Sure,' Elaine said. 'Teresita and Cliff are the year's most heartwarming sight—but marriage?' She shook her head. 'I don't think so. Do you imagine that guardian of hers is going to allow her to throw herself away on a mere chemical engineer?'

'Perhaps he won't care,' said Nicola. 'After all, he doesn't take a great deal of interest in her. He never comes to see her—which is just as well under the circumstances—and his letters are few and far between.'

'True, but that doesn't mean he won't get good and interested if she plans to marry someone he doesn't approve of.'

'But why shouldn't he approve of Cliff? Apart from being one of the nicest guys you could wish to meet, he's well qualified, has a good job, and is more than able to support a wife.'

Elaine shrugged. 'I have a feeling that he'll need a lot more than that to be acceptable as husband material for Teresita. Just consider—since we've known her, how many paying jobs has she had?'

'Only one,' Nicola acknowledged. 'The couple of weeks she spent here as receptionist.'

'Right,' said Elaine. 'And were we surprised that other offers didn't come her way—considering that as a receptionist she was a walking, talking disaster area?'

Nicola grinned, remembering the mislaid messages, misunderstandings, and interrupted telephone calls which had distinguished Teresita's brief sojourn at the reception desk. No one had the least idea how she had ever got the job while the regular girl was on holiday, or how she had lasted in it for longer than five minutes, although Elaine had commented that the management had probably been too dazed by the whole experience to fire her.

'No, we weren't in the least surprised,' she said, and hesitated. 'But she does work.'

'Social work—with the nuns—unpaid,' Elaine pointed out. 'And very estimable too. So, where does she get the money to pay her share of the rent, and buy all those gorgeous clothes that she has—all those little numbers from the boutiques in the Zona Rosa? Not to mention her jewellery.'

'What about her jewellery? It's rather flamboyant, but . . .'

'It's entitled to be flamboyant. It's also real,' Elaine said drily.

There was a small, shaken silence then Nicola said, 'You must be joking.'

'I promise I'm not. I have an uncle who's a jeweller in Santa Barbara, and I spent some of my formative years learning to pick the fake from the real stuff. I'm not making any mistake.'

'My God!' Nicola put her hands to her face. 'She lent me—she actually lent me her pearls that time we all went out to dinner.'

'I remember,' Elaine nodded. 'They looked good on you.'

'That isn't the point,' Nicola almost wailed. 'Suppose I'd lost them—or they'd been stolen?'

'You didn't, and they weren't, and they'll be insured anyway,' Elaine said reasonably. 'But we're getting away from the subject here. What I'm saying is that Teresita isn't just a nice girl we met, who shares our apartment and cooks up the greatest *enchiladas* in Mexico. She's also a rich lady, and if this guardian of hers knows what he's doing, he'll want to marry her money to more money, because that's the way things are, so Cliff and she may have some problems. That's all.'

It was enough, Nicola thought unhappily. She said, 'Teresita's of age, so there's nothing to stop her getting married, if she wants to, and she does want to.'

'Don't sound so fierce! Okay, so she and Cliff are Romeo and Juliet all over again, and she is a very sweet gentle girl. No one would argue. But she's led a very sheltered life. She was practically brought up by nuns, after all, and she'd still be living in that hostel if we hadn't invited her to move in with us. I'm amazed that she ever agreed anyway, and she still trails round to the convent to see if there's any mail for her each day because she's scared her guardian may find out that she's left—because basically she knows in her heart that if he cracks the whip she'll jump, whether she's of age or not.' She paused, giving Nicola a quizzical look. 'And if she dare not tell him she's sharing an apartment in a good part of town with a couple of *gringas*, then just how is she going to break the news that she's engaged to a *norteamericano*?'

'It's rather different,' Nicola argued. 'If he'd forbidden her to leave the hostel, she'd have been unhappy perhaps, but it wouldn't have been the end of the world. But if he makes any objection to her marrying Cliff, then it will break her heart. She might have yielded to pressure over the apartment issue, but not over Cliff. I'm sure of it.'

'Well, you have a touching faith in her will power which I don't share.' Elaine turned back to her paper-shredding. 'I guess we'd better get on with the packing. The place already looks as if we'd moved out.'

'Yes,' said Nicola with a little sigh.

She hadn't expected to enjoy her stay with Trans-Chem. She knew very little about the technicalities of chemical plants and their construction and was happy in her ignorance. She'd just been desperate for some kind of contract which would take her away from Zurich, and ensure that she wasn't there to see Ewan marry the stolid blonde daughter of his company chairman.

Nor had she really expected to get the job, although she knew that the fact that she already spoke Spanish, garnered from an intensive course at the Polytechnic where she'd undergone her secretarial training, would stand her in good stead. Trans-Chem were after all an American company, and most of their personnel were recruited in the States, as Elaine had been.

But the job was offered to her, and she accepted with a growing excitement which helped to alleviate some of the pain and humiliation Ewan had made her suffer. She had fallen so deeply in love with him that it seemed impossible for him not to share her feelings. In fact, he did share them. He admitted as much, but it made no difference to his plans. Ewan intended to marry well, and a mere secretary earning her own living didn't fill the bill as a potential bride at all. Although he did have other plans for her, as Nicola had shamingly discovered when finally he had been forced to tell her that his marriage to Greta was imminent.

She'd sat in the circle of his arms, feeling as if she'd been turned to stone, while part of her mind registered incredulously that he was telling her that his marriage needn't make any difference, that it could even be an advantage. When the promotion which his future father-in-law had promised as a certainty finally materialised, then he would have Nicola transferred to his office as his own secretary. There would be business trips which they would make together, he'd said, and he would help her to find a bigger flat where they could be together as often as possible.

She sat there in silence, listening to his voice, to the confidence in it as he made his sordid plans, and wondered why he should have thought she would ever agree to any such thing, when they had never even been lovers in the generally accepted sense. She had often asked herself what had held her back from that ultimate commitment, and could find no answer except perhaps that there had always been a deep, barely acknowledged instinct which she had obeyed, warning her not to trust too blindly, or to give herself without that trust.

When she was able to think more rationally about what had happened, she knew she ought to feel relief that she hadn't that particular bitterness to add to her disillusionment, but it had seemed cold comfort then, and still did.

She had come to Mexico determined not to make a fool of herself again, and her bitterness had been her shield, not merely against the Mexican men whose persistent attempts to flirt with her had at first annoyed and later amused her, but also against the mainly male American staff of Trans-Chem, many of whom would have shown more than a passing interest in her, if she had allowed them to.

Sometimes she wished she could be more like Elaine, who uninhibitedly enjoyed a series of casual relationships, and wept no tears when they were over. Nicola was aware that some of the men had privately dubbed her 'Snow Queen', and although it had stung a little at the time, she had come to welcome the nickname as a form of protection.

What she hadn't realised was that some men, observing the curve of tawny hair falling to her shoulders, the green eyes with their long fringe of lashes, the small straight nose, and the wilful line of the mouth, would still be sufficiently attracted to find her determined coolness a turn-on, forcing her to an open cruelty which she wouldn't have been capable of before Ewan came into her life.

'My God,' Elaine said once. 'You don't fool around when you're giving someone the brush-off! Poor Craig has gone back to the States convinced he has terminal halitosis.'

Nicola flushed. 'I can't help it. I try to make it clear that I'm not interested, and then they get persistent, so what can I do?'

'You could try saying yes for once.' Elaine gave her a measuring look. 'Whatever went wrong in Zurich, sooner or later some guy's going to come along and make you forget all about it, only you have to give him a chance.'

'Perhaps,' Nicola said woodenly. 'But I can promise you that it's no one I've met so far.'

Probably there never would be anyone, she thought. She was on her guard now. Indeed, she had sometimes wondered if she would have fallen for Ewan quite so hard if she hadn't been confused and lonely, away from home for the first time.

Travelling, seeing the world, had always been her own idea ever since childhood, and her parents, recognising the wanderlust they did not share, had given her the loving encouragement she needed. Her undoubted gift for languages had been the original spur, and she was fluent in French and German before she had left school.

Nicola wondered sometimes where the urge to travel had come from. Her parents were so serenely content on their farm at Barton Abbas in Somerset. It was their world, and they needed nothing better, no matter how much they might enjoy her letters and photographs and stories of faraway places. And Robert, her younger brother, was the same. One day the farm would be his, and that would be enough for him too. But not for her. Never for her.

Now, she wasn't altogether sure what she wanted. Working for Trans-Chem had been more enjoyable than she could ever have anticipated. The company expected high standards of efficiency, but at the same time treated her with a friendly informality which she had never experienced in any previous job, and certainly not in Zurich. And they had been keen, as their contract to assist in a consultative capacity with the building of a new plant in Mexico's expanding chemical industry began to wind up, for her to work for them in the States on a temporary basis at least.

Nicola didn't really know why she'd refused. Certainly she had nothing better in mind, and there would have been no problem in fitting in her longed-for and saved-for sightseeing tour first. Yet refuse she did, and for no better reason than that she felt oddly restless.

Perhaps it was the anticipation of her holiday which was making her feel this way. The last months had been hectic, and the past few weeks of clearing out the office and packing up especially so.

She would miss Elaine, she thought. She'd been a little taken aback when she first arrived in Mexico City to find that she had a readymade flatmate waiting for her. How did she know that she and this tall redhaired Californian were ever going to get along well enough to share a home? And yet from the very first day, they'd had no real problems. And then, later, Teresita had made three . . .

Nicola smiled to herself. Had there ever been a more oddly assorted trio? she wondered. Elaine with her cool laconic humour, and relaxed enjoyment of life, Teresita the wealthy orphan, shy and gentle and almost morbidly in awe of the guardian she never saw—and Nicola herself, a mass of hang-ups, as Elaine had once not unkindly remarked.

In some way, Nicola almost envied Teresita. At least she had few doubts about the world and her place in it. Her upbringing in the seclusion of the convent school had been geared to readying her for marriage, and a subservient role in a male-dominated society. The purpose of her life was to be someone's wife and the mother of his children, and she seemed to accept that as a matter of course.

Even her one small act of rebellion against her strictly ordered existence, her decision to move into the apartment with Nicola and Elaine, had contributed towards her chosen destiny, because without it, it was unlikely that her relationship with Cliff Arnold could have prospered.

They had met during Teresita's brief but eventful spell at the Trans-Chem reception desk. Cliff had been one of many finding himself suddenly cut off in the middle of an important call, and he had erupted into the reception area looking for someone to murder, then stopped, as someone remarked later, as if he'd been poleaxed, as he looked down into Teresita's heart-shaped face, and listened to her huskily voiced apologies. His complaints forgotten, he had spent the next half hour, and many more after that, showing her how to operate the switchboard.

As Elaine had caustically commented, it had improved nothing, but at least they'd had a good time.

Cliff had been a constant visitor at the apartment after Teresita moved in. He had adapted without apparent difficulty to the demands of an old-fashioned courtship, bringing gifts—bottles of wine, bunches of flowers, and once even a singing bird in a cage. Teresita sang too, all round the apartment, small happy songs betokening the inner radiance which showed in her shining eyes and flushed cheeks.

That was how love should be, Nicola thought, bringing its own certainty and security, imposing its welcome obligations. Perhaps it was the constant exposure to Teresita's transparent happiness which was making her so restless. Not that there'd been much radiance about lately, she reminded herself drily. Cliff had been sent to Chicago for a few weeks and in his absence Teresita had drooped like a neglected flower. But he was due to return during the next few days, and Nicola was sure they would be announcing their engagement at the very least as soon as he came back.

That was if Teresita managed to break the news to her guardian, the remote and austere Don Luis Alvarado de Montalba. She seemed very much in awe of him, reluctant even to mention his name, but Nicola had still gleaned a certain amount of information about him.

He was wealthy and powerful, that went without saying. At one time, his family had owned vast cattle estates in the north, but later they had begun to diversify, to invest in industry and in fruit and coffee plantations, apparently foreseeing the time when the huge ranches would be broken up into smaller units and the landowners' monopolies broken.

Not that any government-inspired reforms seemed to have made a great deal of difference to the Montalbas, she thought. They still owned the ranch, although its size had been reduced, as well as a town house in Monterrey where much of their industrial interest was concentrated, and a luxurious villa near Acapulco. Nicola gathered that Teresita's father had been a business colleague of Don Luis, and this was why she had been assigned to his guardianship after her parents had been tragically drowned in a flash-flood some years before.

Clearly, his guardianship operated more on a financial and business level than a personal one. Teresita had admitted candidly that it was over a year since he had visited her, and she seemed more relieved than otherwise at this state of affairs.

Clearly he was the type of aloof and imposing grandee who would be incapable of putting a young girl at her ease, Nicola thought. Teresita always behaved as if even to talk about him was a form of *lèse-majeste*.

Nicola could just picture him—elderly with heavy moustaches, perhaps even a beard, probably overweight, pompous and arrogant. She hoped fervently that Elaine was wrong and he wouldn't make an attempt to interfere in Teresita's happiness. There was no reason why he should, she thought. Cliff was no fortune-hunter, even if he didn't have the sort of wealth that the Montalba family had at its disposal.

She fastened the last carton, sealed and labelled it, then sat back on her heels with a sigh.

'So that's done. I could do with a cup of coffee. Do you think the machine's still working?'

'If so it's the only thing in the building that is, apart from us,' said Elaine. 'In my next life, I'm coming back as a boss. You finish up here, and I'll go see about this coffee.'

She was gone for some time, and Nicola guessed that the machine, never enthusiastic about its function at the best of times, had finally given up the ghost and that Elaine had called to buy coffee at the small restaurant a few doors away.

She wandered over to the window and stood looking down into the square. The noise of the traffic seemed muted in the midday heat and from the street below she could hear the plaintive strains of a barrel-organ. The organ-grinder was there most days, and she knew his repertoire almost by heart, but today the jangling notes seemed to hold an extra poignancy, and she felt unbidden tears start to her eyes.

She was being a fool she told herself. What had she got to cry about? She'd had a marvellous time in Mexico City, and within a few days she would be embarking on the holiday of a lifetime. Unlike Elaine she had always been fascinated by the history of the New World, and her tour had been carefully planned to take in as many of the great archeological sites as possible. She found herself saying some of the names under her breath—Palenque, Uxmal, Chichen Itza. Great pyramids, towering temples, ancient pagan gods—she'd dreamed of such things, and soon, very soon, all her dreams would come true. So why in hell was she standing here snivelling? She heard the outer door open and slam in the corridor, and turned hastily, smearing the tears from her face with clumsy fingers, hoping that Elaine would not notice or be too tactful to comment.

As the office door crashed open, she made herself smile.

'You've been long enough,' she began teasingly. 'Did you have to pick the beans personally or . . .'

She stopped short, her eyes widening in disbelief as she studied the dishevelled, woebegone figure in front of her.

'Teresita!' she gasped. '*Querida*, what is it? Has something happened? Are you ill?' Her heart sank as she saw Teresita's brimming eyes. 'Cliff—oh, my God, has something happened to Cliff?'

'No,' Teresita said. 'He is well—he is fine—and I shall never see him again.' And she burst into hysterical tears.

Nicola had got her into a chair and was trying to calm her when Elaine returned with two paper cups of coffee.

'I guess I should have brought something stronger,'

she remarked as she put the cups down on the nearest desk. 'What's wrong?'

'I wish I knew.' Nicola scrabbled through drawers until she came across a box of tissues in the last one. 'All she keeps saying is that she wants to die, and begging our Lady of Guadeloupe to take her.'

Elaine raised her brows. 'Clearly, she means business. Talk to her in Spanish, Nicky. She may make more sense that way.'

Nicola mustered her thoughts and said crisply 'Stop crying, Teresita. If we can help you we will, but first we must understand why you're so distressed.'

Teresita was still sobbing, but she was making an effort to control herself. When she spoke, Nicola could just make out the whispered words, 'I am to be married.'

'Yes, we know that.' Nicola passed her another tissue. 'To Cliff, just as soon as it can be arranged—so what is there to cry about?'

Teresita shook her head. 'It is not so.' Her voice was steadying, becoming more coherent. 'Today I visited the convent to pray in the chapel for Cliff's safe return. The Reverend Mother, she tells me there is a letter for me, and I see at once it is from my guardian, Don Luis. I read the letter. *Madre de Dios*, I read it and I wish only to die!'

'You mean he's forbidden you to marry Cliff?' Nicola asked sharply.

'He does not yet know that Cliff exists,' Teresita said bleakly. 'Always I have waited for the right time to tell him, because I feared his anger.'

'Will someone please fill me in on what's going on?' Elaine demanded plaintively.

'I wish I knew myself,' said Nicola, hurriedly outlining the gist of the conversation so far.

'It's obviously this letter,' Elaine said. She crouched beside Teresita's chair, taking her hands in hers. 'Hey, honey, what was in the letter? Does the mighty Don Luis want you to marry someone else? Is that it?'

Choking back a sob, Teresita nodded, and Elaine darted Nicola a sober glance which said 'I told you so' more clearly and loudly than any words could have done.

'Tomorrow,' Teresita said. 'Tomorrow I must leave Mexico City and travel to Monterrey with Ramón. Later we shall be married.'

'You and this Ramón? Just like that?' Nicola demanded, horrified.

Teresita's eyes widened. 'Not Ramón, no. He is just the cousin of Don Luis. I met him once when I was a child.'

'For heaven's sake,' Elaine muttered, and Nicola said hastily, 'I'm sorry, darling, we're trying to understand. But if Ramón isn't the bridegroom then who . . .?'

'It is Don Luis.' Teresita's voice was flat.

Nicola muttered 'My God!' and Elaine's lips pursed in a silent whistle.

'Nice one, Don Luis,' she approved. 'Nothing like keeping the cash where it belongs—in the family.'

'It is what my father intended. I have always known this,' Teresita said tonelessly. 'But, as time passed, and he said nothing, I began to hope that it would never happen. A man so much older than myself, a man who has known so many women.' For a moment, a world of knowledge that the good nuns had never instilled showed on the heart-shaped face. 'I—I allowed myself to hope that perhaps he would choose elsewhere—perhaps even marry Carlota Garcia.'

'Just who is that?' Elaine asked.

Teresita gave a slight shrug. 'A—a friend of his. Her husband was a politician. She has been a widow now for several years, and their names have been coupled together many times. A girl—one of the boarders at the convent—told me it was known that she was his— *amiga*. She said it was impossible that he would marry me because I was too much of a child for him, accustomed as he is to women of the world.'

Disgust rose bitterly in Nicola. Not just elderly and arrogant, but mercenary and a womaniser into the bargain.

She said hotly, 'You can't marry him, Teresita. Write to him. Tell him it's all off. He can't make you.'

Teresita almost cowered in her chair. 'I cannot disobey.' Her voice shook. 'Tomorrow I must leave for Monterrey in Ramón's charge. You do not know Don Luis—his anger—how he would be if I wrote him such a letter.'

'But he must know that you don't love him—that you're even frightened of him,' Nicola argued stubbornly.

Teresita sighed. 'My mother would have said that it is a good thing to respect the man that one must marry—and that love can follow marriage,' she added doubtfully.

'When you already love Cliff?'

Teresita's mouth quivered. 'That was craziness, a dream. I must forget him now that Don Luis has spoken at last.'

'Oh, no, you mustn't,' Nicola said forcefully. 'Teresita, you can't let yourself be pushed around like this. Your father may have intended you to marry Don Luis at one time, but if he was here now, and knew Cliff, and realised how you felt about him, I know he'd change his mind.' She looked across at Elaine, who gave a silent shrug. She tried again. 'Why don't you and Cliff elope?'

For a moment, a hopeful light shone in Teresita's eyes, then she crumpled again.

'He is in Chicago.'

'Well, I know that, but we could cable him, tell him it's an emergency and he has to get back right away,' said Nicola.

Teresita shook her head. 'I must leave tomorrow. There is no time for him to return.'

'Then he'll just have to follow you to Monterrey and make Don Luis see reason.'

'It would be no use. Don Luis would not receive him, or allow me to see him.' Teresita spread her hands help-lessly. 'Nicky, you do not understand.'

'On the contrary, I understand only too well,' Nicola told her grimly. 'You're not prepared to stand up to this guardian of yours.'

Teresita seemed to shrink. 'Nicky, it is not possible to stand up, as you say. He follows his own will at all times, and always he is obeyed.'

'Oh, is he, indeed?' Nicola said wrathfully. 'I just wish I could meet this lordly gentleman. I'd do any-thing to stop him getting his own way for once in his life!'

'Then why don't you?' said Elaine.

'Why don't I what?'

'Stop him.' Elaine gave a shrug. 'Correct me if I'm wrong, Teresita, but you're not very well acquainted with this Ramón, are you?'

'No.' Teresita gave a puzzled frown. 'As I said, he is Don Luis' cousin, and many years ago I met him at La Mariposa and . . .'

'Right,' Elaine interrupted. 'And all he knows is that tomorrow he has to collect you someplace—the convent, I guess—and escort you to Monterrey. Well, Nicky can go in your place.'

There was a shaken silence, then Nicola said, 'That's the silliest idea I've ever heard.'

'It's not so silly,' Elaine said calmly. 'Stop and think. You speak Spanish like a native, and if we fitted you out with a brunette wig, some dark glasses and a heavier make-up, you could pass for Teresita—especially with a guy who saw her once when she was a kid, for God's sake.'

Nicola gasped, 'But I'd never get away with it! Just supposing I could fool this unfortunate man—which is by no means certain—what would happen when I got to Monterrey? I couldn't hope for the same luck with Don Luis.'

'You wouldn't need it. You take your big leather shoulder bag in which you have one of your own dresses, and your papers and vacation tickets. When you get to Monterrey, you make some excuse to stop off some-where—a store or a restaurant, and you go to the powder room, where you take off the wig and dump it, change your dress—and—*voilà*. Goodbye, Teresita Dominguez and hello, Nicola Tarrant, leaving Don Luis with egg on his face because his *novia* has run away. Oh, he'll be looking for her, but he won't be equating her with any blonde English chick, and he won't be searching in Mexico City, where she'll be marrying Cliff, with me as chief bridesmaid. When she's ready, she can write and tell him she's already married, and let him figure out how she did it.'

Nicola was about to tell Elaine that this time she had finally flipped, when she saw Teresita looking at her, with the dawning of a wild hope in her eyes.

She said, 'Teresita, no—I couldn't! It's crazy. It's impossible. It wouldn't work.'

Teresita's hands were clasped tightly in front of her as if she were praying. 'But we could make it work, Nicky, in a wig, as Elaine said, and some of my clothes. It will take two days, maybe even three to drive to Monterrey, because there are business calls which Ramón must make on the way for my guardian. Then when you reach Monterrey, there could be at least one more day while Don Luis searches there . . .' She turned eagerly to Elaine, who nodded.

'We'll cable Cliff right away,' she said. 'Maybe Nicky could play for time in other ways on the trip—pretend to be sick or something.'

'I wouldn't have to pretend,' Nicola said desperately. 'Stop it, the pair of you. You're mad!'

Elaine gave her a steady look. 'You said you'd do anything to stop this happening. What Teresita chiefly needs is time—time for Cliff to get back here and marry her himself—and this you could give her.'

'Yes,' Teresita said with a little sob. 'Oh, yes, Nicky. If I go to Monterrey, then I shall never see Cliff again. I know it.'

'But I really don't think I could get away with it,' Nicola said, trying to hold on to her sanity. 'Oh, I know people congratulate me on my fluency and my accent, but all it would need would be one small mistake and I'd be finished. And I can hardly drive hundreds of miles in stony silence.'

'But why not? Ramon would not expect me, the *novia* of his cousin, to talk and chatter to him. It would be *indecoroso*. And if you pretended that the motion of the car was making you ill, then he would not expect you to speak at all. He is much younger than Don Luis, and when I was a child, he was kind to me.' She was silent for a moment, then she said pleadingly, 'Nicky, I beg you to do this thing for me. I could not love Don Luis, and he does not love me. He marries me only because it is time he was married, and because he wishes for a son to inherit this new—empire that he has made. Would you, in your heart, wish to be married for such a reason?'

Nicola was very still. As if it was yesterday, she saw Ewan smiling at her, and heard his voice. 'Of course I'm not in love with her, darling. It's you I care about. But Greta knows what the score is. She understands these things. Once I've married her, there's no reason why you and I shouldn't be together as much as we want, as long as we're discreet.'

She suppressed a little shudder, remembering how, even through the agony of the moment, there had been a flash of pity for Ewan's wife, who would never possess the certainty of his love and loyalty. A marriage of convenience, she had thought bitterly. Very convenient for the man—but heartbreak for the woman.

Teresita didn't deserve such a fate.

She said, 'All right, I'll do it.'

CHAPTER TWO

NICOLA stood nervously in the shadow of the portico and stared down the quiet and empty street. Ramón was late, and at any moment the door behind could open and one of the nuns emerge, and ask what she was doing there.

For the umpteenth time she had to resist the impulse to adjust the wig. It was a loathsome thing, totally realistic, but hot and itchy. Orchid pink silky dress, strapped sandals with high heels in a matching kid, and two of Teresita's expensive cases as window dressing. The only thing out of place was the bulky leather bag on her shoulder, but it would just have to look incongruous. It was her lifeline.

She glanced at her watch, biting her lip nervously, thinking how funny it would be if it was all for nothing and Don Luis had changed his mind—and then she saw the car and her stomach lurched in panic.

It was too late now to run for it. She could only cross her fingers that the wig and cosmetics and the large pair of dark glasses would be sufficiently convincing. Swallowing, she adopted an air of faint hauteur as Teresita had suggested and stared in front of her as the car came to a halt in front of the convent steps.

There was a uniformed chauffeur at the wheel, but Nicola barely registered the fact. She was too busy looking at the man who had just emerged from the front passenger seat and was standing by the car watching her.

Young, Teresita had said, or at least younger than Don Luis. Well, he was at least in his mid-thirties, so that figured, but what she hadn't mentioned, either because she'd forgotten or had been too young to notice, was that Ramon was a disturbingly, even devastatingly, attractive man. Tall—unusually so—with black hair, and eyes darker than sin. Golden bronze skin over a classic bone structure that went beyond conventional good looks. A high-bridged aristocratic nose, a firm-lipped mouth, the purity of its lines betrayed only by a distinctly unchaste curve to his lower lip, and a proudly uncompromising strength of chin.

'Ye gods,' Nicola thought, 'and this is only the poor relation! What the Mark II model is like makes the mind reel.' Somehow the image of the plump, pompous gran-dee didn't seem quite so valid any more.

He walked forward, strong shoulders, lean hips and long legs encased in a lightweight but very expensive suit. His black silk shirt was open at the throat, allowing a glimpse of smooth brown chest.

He was smiling faintly, and Nicola thought, her hackles rising, that he was clearly under no illusion about his effect on women.

'Señorita.' He stood at the foot of the steps and looked up at her rather enquiringly.

'I am Teresita Dominguez, señor,' she said coldly. 'And you are late.'

Now that the words were uttered, and the charade begun, it was somehow easier.

If Don Luis had informed his cousin that his future wife was a submissive doormat of a girl who would speak when spoken to, then Don Ramón de Costanza had just had the shock of his life, she thought with satisfaction. She was pleased to see that he did look taken aback.

'My apologies, Señorita Dominguez. I was detained. And of course I could not know—I was not warned what a vision of loveliness awaited me.'

No one warned me about you either, she thought silently. And Don Luis must be off his head to let you out of your cage to prowl round the girl he's going to marry, cousin or no cousin.

She primmed her mouth disapprovingly as he came up the steps to her side. 'Don Ramón, must I remind you who I am?'

'Indeed no, *señorita*. You are the *novia* of Don Luis Alvarado de Montalba, the most fortunate man in Mexico. Welcome to our family, Teresita—if I may call you that?' He lifted her hand as if to kiss it lightly, then at the last moment turned it over, and brushed his mouth swiftly and sensuously across the palm instead.

'*Señor*.' Nicola snatched her hand away, aware that she did not have to pretend the note of shock in her voice. Her flesh tingled as if it had been in contact with a live electric current. 'I hope I do not have to inform Don Luis of your behaviour.'

'Forgive me.' He didn't sound particularly repentant. 'I forgot myself. You will have nothing further to complain of in my conduct, I swear. Will you allow me to put your cases in the car?'

She assented with a cool nod, and followed him down the steps, her heart still thumping.

'And your bag?'

She swallowed, shaking her head and taking a firm hold on the strap.

'I prefer to keep it with me.'

He surveyed the bag in silence for a moment. 'It lacks the charm and elegance of the rest of your appearance.'

'It has sentimental value,' she said shortly.

'I'm glad it has something,' he said smoothly. The chauffeur was holding the rear door open, and she climbed in, taking pains to do so without displaying too much leg. The door was shut and she saw her travelling companion detain the man with a hand on his arm and tell him something which clearly caused the chauffeur some surprise before he nodded and turned away.

The next minute Ramón came round and also got in the back of the car beside her. She saw the chauffeur watching covertly in the mirror, his face deliberately stolid and expressionless.

Keep your eyes on that mirror, *amigo*, she addressed him silently, and if he puts a hand on me anywhere, call in the army.

She leaned back in her seat, forcing herself to relax, reminding herself that she was occupying a very spacious, luxurious air-conditioned vehicle, and the fact that it felt crowded was purely imaginary.

The car began to move, and she felt tiny beads of perspiration break out on her top lip. They were on their way. So far so good, she thought, then stole a glance at her travelling companion and realised that there was absolutely no room for complacency on this journey. And she had promised Teresita that she would use delaying tactics, and make it last as long as possible. She swallowed, and turned her attention as resolutely as possible to the scenery outside the car.

They had been travelling for over half an hour when he said, 'You are very quiet.'

It was her chance. She produced a lace-trimmed handkerchief from her bag, and dabbed her lips with it.

'I am not a good traveller, Don Ramón. You must excuse me.'

She hiccuped realistically, and settled further into her corner of the seat, relishing the slightly alarmed expression on his face. She closed her eyes and pretended to doze, and eventually pretence was overtaken by reality, and, lulled by the smooth motion of the car, she slept.

She awoke with a start some time later. Her eyes flew open and she saw that he was watching her, the dark face curiously hard and speculative. As she looked at him uncertainly, the expression faded, and there was nothing but that former charm.

'Welcome back, *señorita*. Are you feeling better?'

She said, 'A little,' and sat up, her hands automatically smoothing some of the creases out of the skirt of her dress. His eyes followed her movements, observing the rounded shape of her thighs beneath the clinging material, and she flushed slightly, thankful that her bag was on the seat between them, an actual physical barricade.

'Where are we?' They seemed to be passing through a town. He mentioned a name, but it meant nothing.

'I had intended to stop here for lunch,' he said, after a pause. 'But as you are unwell, perhaps it would be unwise.'

Nicola groaned inwardly. She could hardly confess the truth, that she was starving. Tension seemed to be giving her an appetite.

'Please don't let my indisposition interfere with your plans, Don Ramón,' she said meekly. 'While you eat, I can always go for a walk. The—the fresh air might do me good.'

Again she was conscious of the speculative stare, then he said, 'As you wish, *señorita*.'

The chauffeur, whose name was Lopez, parked in a small square behind the church.

Ramón helped her out. 'Are you sure you will be all right?' He paused. 'It is only a small place, you can hardly get lost.'

'I'll be fine,' she assured him, reaching for the strap of her bag.

'You don't wish to take that heavy thing with you. Leave it in the car,' he suggested.

Rather at a loss, she said, 'I'm used to carrying it. It—it doesn't worry me.'

'Clearly you are not as frail as you seem,' he murmured.

She waited to see what direction he took with Lopez, and made sure she went the other way. In one of the streets off the square a small market was in full swing, and there were food stalls, she saw thankfully. Black bean soup, she decided with relish, and *sopes* to follow. She had learned to love the little corn dough boats filled with chili and topped with cheese and vegetables and spiced sausage which were to be found cooking on griddles at so many roadside foodstalls. She ate every scrap, and licked her fingers.

She felt far more relaxed, and in a much better temper as she sauntered back to the car. Ramón de Costanza was standing outside the car, looking at his watch and tapping his foot with impatience as she approached.

'I wondered if I would have to come and find you,' he said silkily. 'Did you enjoy your stroll?'

'*Gracias, señor*. Did you enjoy your lunch?'

'It was delicious.' He looked faintly amused as he surveyed her and Nicola wondered uneasily whether she had left any traces of black bean soup round her mouth.

As he took his seat beside her in the car, Ramon said, 'I have a business call to make a few kilometres ahead, and then we will find somewhere to stay for the night.'

'Already?' she asked with a frown.

He looked surprised. 'It will soon be the time for *siesta*. You don't want to continue our journey through the full heat of the day, or ask Lopez to do so.'

'No, of course not,' she said, feeling a fool. 'I—I wasn't thinking.' That had to count as a slip, she thought. Surely by now she should be used to the way life in Mexico slowed to a crawl in the late afternoon. She was taking too much for granted, losing her edge, and it couldn't happen again, or he might begin to suspect.

They eventually arrived at a motel, a large rambling white building surrounded by lush gardens, fountains and even a swimming pool. Nicola stared at it longingly, and then banished even the thought regretfully. Ladies wearing wigs stayed on dry land. Besides, her bikinis were all in her own cases on the way to Merida by now, and that was just as well, because the prospect of appearing before Ramón de Costanza so scantily clad was an alarming one.

Every time she had as much as glanced in his direction, he had been watching her, she thought broodingly.

And that was putting it mildly. What he had actually been doing was undressing her with his eyes, and in her role as Teresita she couldn't even make a protest, because the innocent Teresita wouldn't have known for one moment what he was doing.

But I know, she thought, grinding her teeth, and longing to embed the delicate heel of her sandal in his shin.

The cabin to which she was shown was spotlessly clean and comfortable, with a tiny tiled bathroom opening off the bedroom. She turned to close the door and found Ramón on her heels. He gave the room an appraising look, which also encompassed the wide bed under its cream coverlet. Then he turned to her, taking her hand and lifting it up to his lips.

'A pleasant *siesta*. You have everything you need?' He looked straight into her eyes, and with a sudden rush of painful and unwelcome excitement she realised she had only to make the slightest sign and the door would be locked, closing them in together.

She snatched her hand away, seeing the mockery in his eyes.

'Everything, thank you, *señor*,' she said in a stiff little voice.

'Can I hope for the pleasure of your company later at dinner?'

She gave him a cool smile and said that it would be very nice. When he had gone, she turned the key in the lock herself. She wanted to collapse limply across the bed, but first she took off the orchid pink dress, and the wig. She saw herself in the mirror across the room. Except for the slightly heavier make-up, she was herself again. She ran her fingers through her sticky hair and moved towards the bathroom. As she did so, she had to pass the bed, and just for a moment she let the tight rein she kept on herself slacken a little and wondered what would have happened if she had given him the signal he wanted—a smile would have been enough, she thought, or even the faintest pressure of her fingers in his.

And just for a moment her imagination ran wild, and he was there in the bed waiting for her, his golden skin dramatically dark against the pale sheets, his eyes caressing her as she moved towards him.

She stopped the pictures unrolling in her mind right there with an immense effort of will.

Then she said, 'Hell,' quite viciously, and went to have her shower.

She had managed to recover her composure by the time she was due to join him in the dining room. She was wearing a simple dark red dress with black high-heeled court shoes, and a small evening bag. Her precious leather holdall was safely stowed in the closet.

The verandah bar outside the motel restaurant was crowded with people, many of them tourists, but she saw him at once. He was sitting at a table near the verandah rail, with a glass in his hand, and he was frowning. Nicola noticed wryly that a party of American women at the next table couldn't take their eyes off him.

She threaded her way through the other tables, and joined him. *'Buenas tardes, señor.'* She meant to sound cool, but only succeeded in being shy. He rose immediately, holding a chair for her to sit down and summoning a waiter with a swift imperious flick of his fingers. She asked for a *tamarindo* and it came at once.

She sipped, relishing the coolness of the drink and its faintly bitter flavour.

'Tell me,' he said, 'those dark glasses—surely you don't need them in the evening. I hope there is nothing the matter with your eyes.'

'Oh, no,' she said calmly. 'I've just been advised to wear them all the time for a short while.' And that, she thought with satisfaction, was nothing less than the truth.

'A pity,' he said. 'One can learn so much about a woman from her eyes.'

She said sweetly, 'And about a man, *señor*.'

His mouth quivered slightly. 'As you say,' he agreed.

It was pleasant, looking out into the darkness with the scent of the flowers wafting to them on the night air, and hearing the distant splash of water from the fountains interspersed with the bursts of laughter and conversation all around them. Nicola had to suppress a little sigh. She would have other memories to take with her, apart from ancient pagan artefacts, when she came to leave Mexico. She was conscious of a feeling of recklessness, and decided it would be wiser to stick to fruit juice for the remainder of the evening.

She tried to remember everything Teresita had told her about Ramón. There wasn't a great deal. He lived at the *hacienda* La Mariposa and ran the cattle ranch for his cousin. His mother, Doña Isabella, and his sister Pilar lived there too, and Teresita had said he was 'kind.' Nicola had got the impression that Teresita would not have applied the same epithet to his mother and sister, however, even though there had only been that one meeting all those years ago.

She had asked Teresita why the *hacienda* was called La Mariposa—the Butterfly, but Teresita had simply shrugged vaguely and said it was just a name.

Anyway, what did it matter? Nicola told herself. She wasn't going to the *hacienda*, but to Monterrey, and none of the Montalba residences would be available for her inspection.

She wondered what Ramón would say when she realised how he had been fooled, and whether Don Luis would be very angry with him. She stole a glance at him. The arrogant set of his jaw indicated that he might have quite a temper himself.

It was a delicious meal. He had ordered chicken for them cooked in a sauce made with green peppers and a variety of other tantalising flavours she didn't have time to analyse. And, in spite of her protests, there was wine, one of the regional varieties, cool and heady.

And she sat across the table from him, hiding behind her dark glasses, and weaving silent fantasies where she was no longer playing a part, but was herself, Nicola Tarrant, free to talk, to smile, to laugh and enjoy herself in his company.

Because in spite of her instinctive wariness of him, in spite of the strain of having to maintain a conversation not in her own language, she was enjoying herself. It was a pleasant sensation to encounter covertly envying glances from other women, to notice the deferential service they received from the staff. Some tourists at a nearby table were sampling tequila for the first time, getting in a muddle over the salt and lemon juice amid peals of laughter, and Nicola smiled too as she watched, her fingers toying with the stem of her wineglass. She looked at her companion and saw that he shared her amusement, and the moment seemed to enclose them in a bubble of intimacy. His hand was very near hers. If he moved it as much as an inch, their fingers would brush. Nicola took a deep breath and moved, picking up her glass and pretending to drink.

She was playing a dangerous game with this crazy charade she had embarked upon, but in a way it might prove to be her salvation. As Nicola Tarrant, she could be fatally tempted to respond to any further advances he might make. As Teresita, she could not be.

All the same, she found his attitude a puzzling one. Teresita had given her the impression that Ramón was Don Luis' trusted and highly regarded employee as well as cousin. She would have supposed that under those circumstances he would have treated his cousin's future wife with the greatest respect. Perhaps he was a man who could not resist a flirtation with any attractive woman who crossed his path, she thought, conscious of a vague feeling of disappointment. Or maybe there was some deeper, darker motive for his behaviour. Perhaps he secretly hated Don Luis, or out of loyalty to him was testing his *novia*'s virtue to make sure she was a worthy bride for a Montalba.

She wondered wryly how the shy, unworldly Teresita herself would have made out on this journey. Would she even have recognised the kind boy she remembered from her childhood? Or would the predator in him have been defeated by her gentleness? After all, Cliff had not been a model of rectitude before he began to associate with Teresita, but now he was tenderly protective towards her.

Some musicians had appeared and were moving among the tables, playing guitars and singing. Nicola recognised the tune they were playing. It was a love song, which had been popular in Mexico City only a few weeks earlier, and she began to hum it softly under her breath. The musicians were approaching their table. They had clearly noticed her enjoyment and were coming to continue the serenade just for her. The leader was smiling broadly and looking at her companion, then Nicola noticed his expression change. She sent a swift glance at Ramón and saw that his face had become a dark mask. His fingers made a swift imperious movement, and the *mariachi* band turned away, and serenaded someone else.

She drank her wine, trying to hide her disappointment. A private flirtation conducted in the car was one thing, and a public serenade quite another, apparently.

Pushing back her chair, she said coolly, 'The journey has tired me. I think I will go to my room. Goodnight, *señor.*'

There was faint mockery in his eyes as he rose courteously. 'Of course, *Buenas noches*, Teresita.' There was a brief hesitation before he used her name, as if to emphasise his rejection of her own formality.

She walked away, wondering in spite of herself why he had not offered to see her to her cabin. Perhaps he had decided that it was wiser to call a halt after all, to treat her with appropriate reserve. Probably that was why he had sent away the *mariachi* musicians.

She undressed slowly, and lay for a long time in the dark, tired, but unable to sleep. It was a relief to know that she had to disappear when they reached Monterrey. It was also a warning not to relax, or forget even for a moment what she was doing on this journey. Playing a part, she thought, and playing for time. Nothing else. And it's just as well that I'm committed to vanish completely in a couple of days.

She breakfasted in her room early the following morning, enjoying the sweet rolls and strongly flavoured coffee a maid brought her. Then she dressed and made up with care and went to find Ramón. She found him in the main reception area, just coming out of one of the private telephone booths.

He said coolly, 'Thank you for being so punctual. We have a long and tedious drive ahead of us. I hope you will not be too bored. Was it explained to you that I had business calls to make on the way?'

'Yes.' She was puzzled by this sudden aloofness.

He gave her a swift sideways glance. 'I have been speaking to my cousin. I have a message for you from Don Luis.'

Her heart gave a little panicky jerk. She said, 'Is that so?'

'Don't you want to hear it?'

'No,' she said, 'I do not. If your cousin has anything to say to me, then it can be said when we meet, and not relayed through a third person.'

He said evenly, 'As you wish, *señorita*,' but she saw a muscle flicker in his cheek, and guessed he was annoyed.

This time the journey was very different from that of the previous day. He sat in the back beside her, but there was a briefcase with him and his attention seemed riveted on the papers it contained. There was a distance between them that wasn't purely physical, and today she didn't even need to use her shoulder bag as a barricade.

She sat and stared out of the window at the purple and grey shades of the *sierras* in the distance. This was a region of Mexico she hadn't expected to see, and normally she would have been fascinated by the changing scenery, the unrolling fertile farmlands they were passing through, but she was unable to summon much interest at all.

Nicola bit her lip. She was altogether too distracted by the presence of her fellow-passenger, and while that might have been forgivable the day before when he had apparently been deliberately making her aware of him, there was no excuse at all today when he was doing quite the opposite.

Clearly the conversation with Don Luis had reminded him of his obligations and responsibilities, she thought.

They made several stops on the way. Nicola wondered whether she was expected to remain obediently in the car on each occasion, but the first time Ramón glanced at his watch and said briefly, 'I shall be not longer than twenty minutes,' which seemed to indicate that she was to be left to her own devices.

And yet that was not altogether true, as she discovered when she left the car and stretched her cramped limbs. Ramón had disappeared inside some large official-looking building, and the car was parked between this and a large ornate church.

Nicola strolled towards it and found Lopez behind her. She gave him a cool smile and said that he could remain in the car.

'This is a very small town,' she added ironically. 'I shall not get lost.'

But Lopez was civil yet determined. It was the Señor's wish that he should accompany her, he said, and his tone made it clear that that was that. She was a little disconcerted, to say the least. No watchdog had been considered necessary yesterday, so why today? She visited the church, first tying a scarf over her head as she guessed Teresita would do, then wandered round the streets, examining pottery and fabrics on roadside stalls, and looking in shop windows full of leather goods, but conscious all the time of Lopez' silent presence at her shoulder.

And when the twenty minutes were up, he reminded her politely that they were keeping the Señor waiting.

That, she found to her annoyance, was to be the pattern of the day. The swift and silent drive along the highway, while Ramón read documents and made notes on them, then the brief stopover and the saunter round the neighbouring streets.

At last, exasperated, she said to Ramón, as the car moved off once again, 'Is it on Don Luis' instructions that I'm being taken round the streets like a prisoner under guard?'

He glanced at her. 'I thought you were not interested in his instructions.'

'Am I expected to be?' she demanded. 'For months on end he behaves as if I don't exist, and then on his command I must go here and there, do this and that. What else can he expect but my hostility—and resentment?' she added for good measure, sowing the seeds to provide an explanation for her disappearance in Monterrey.

For a moment he was silent, then his mouth slanted cynically. 'I think you will find that he expects a great deal more than either of those.'

'Then he's going to be be bitterly disappointed,' Nicola snapped. 'Now please call off your sentry!'

She wasn't just acting. She meant it. Having Lopez following her everywhere was going to cause endless difficulties when she eventually made her bid for freedom.

'Don Luis wishes you to be adequately protected,' the even voice said.

'Does he?' she asked bitterly. 'Then perhaps he should

be informed that I'm in far less danger wandering round the towns than I am in this car, Don Ramón!'

He looked at her with open mockery. 'Then why don't you tell him so when you meet him? I am sure he would be fascinated.'

She hunched a shoulder irritably, and turned to stare out of the window, hearing him laugh softly.

'I am glad your travel sickness has not troubled you today,' he said after a pause. 'Perhaps before the trip is over I may also be able to persuade you to remove your glasses.'

Still with her back turned, she said calmly, 'That is quite impossible.'

'We shall see,' he said softly, and she turned and looked at him sharply, only to find he was once more immersed in his papers.

They ate lunch in a hilltop restaurant overlooking a lake. Nicola ate fish, probably caught from the same lake, she thought, and incredibly fresh and delicately flavoured. Ramón ate little, but he drank wine, staring broodingly into the depths of his glass.

She had expected that he would instruct Lopez to stop at a motel again before the siesta hour, but he did not do so. Instead the car sped on through the heat-shimmered landscape, and eventually, lulled by the motion, Nicola dozed.

She awoke eventually with a slight start, aware that she had been dreaming, but not sure what the dreams were about. Until she turned her head slightly, and then she remembered.

In his corner of the car, he was asleep, his lean body totally relaxed. Nicola felt herself draw a deep shaken breath as the memory of her dreams whispered enticingly to her mind. He had discarded his jacket, and his brown shirt was half unbuttoned, showing the dark shadow of hair on his bronzed body. The shirt fitted closely, revealing not an ounce of spare flesh round his midriff or flat stomach.

Nicola moistened dry lips with the tip of her tongue, conscious of a pang of self-disgust. She had never stared obsessively at a man like this, not even Ewan whom she had loved. Still loved, she thought.

She looked back at him slowly, reluctantly. He wasn't her idea of a rancher, she thought. His shoulders were broad, but his body seemed too finely boned. Her eyes drifted downwards over the long legs and strongly muscled thighs—the result, she supposed, of long days in the saddle. Yet his hands were a mystery, not calloused and rough as she would have imagined, but square-palmed with long sensitive fingers.

She caught back a sigh, as her eyes returned to his face, then gasped huskily as she realised too late that he was awake and watching her.

She sat motionless, thanking heavens for the dark glasses which masked any betrayal there might be in her eyes, but her breathing was flurried, and she saw his eyes slide down her body to her breasts, tautly outlined inside her dress, the nipples hard and swollen against the softly clinging fabric. She saw the dark eyes narrow as they assimilated this shaming evidence of her arousal.

He said softly, 'You overwhelm me, *querida*. Shall I tell Lopez to drive further into the hills and lose himself for an hour or two?'

She felt the hot rush of colour into her face. She wanted to die.

She said icily, 'You are insulting, *señor*.'

'I thought I was being practical.'

'Your vile suggestions are an outrage!' she accused, her voice shaking.

'Of course.' He smiled slightly. 'What a lot you will have to tell Don Luis—when you meet him.'

'You can even think of him?'

'I have been thinking of him a great deal,' he said coolly. 'And always with you, naked and more than willing in his arms, *querida*. A disturbing vision, believe me.'

Her lips parted, then closed again helplessly. Nicola couldn't think of a single word to say, but she knew she had to say something, for Teresita's sake. Although there was no way Teresita would have ever got into this situation, she realised despairingly. She couldn't really believe that she herself had done such a thing.

She said haughtily, 'Please do not speak to me again, Don Ramón.'

It was weak, but it was the best she could manage. She turned her back on him resolutely and stared out of the window, totally unseeing, praying that the blush which seemed to be eating her alive would soon subside.

She couldn't think what was wrong with her. She wasn't completely unsophisticated. He'd made a verbal pass, that was all. It wasn't the end of the world. It had happened to her before, and she'd demolished the perpetrator without a second thought. She was Nicola Tarrant, the Snow Queen, who could cut a too ardent male down with a scornful look. She had never fluttered or flustered in her life, and especially not over the past year. And it wasn't enough to tell herself that her outrage was assumed, part of the role she was playing. She was shaken to the core, and she knew it.

When the car finally stopped, she almost stumbled out of it, barely aware that they were at yet another motel, but smaller this time and far less luxurious. She knew that Lopez was watching her curiously, and tried desperately to pull herself together and act normally.

Ramón came to her side. 'Will you have dinner with me?' His voice sounded constrained.

She avoided his gaze. 'No—I have a headache. I'll ask for some food to be sent to my room.'

'As you please.' He made no attempt to detain her, and she fled. Safe in her room, she made no attempt to order any food, knowing that she wouldn't be able to swallow as much as a morsel. She undressed and showered and lay down on top of the bed, staring into the gathering darkness, her whirling thoughts refusing to cohere into any recognisable pattern.

There was one rock to hang on to in her sea of confusion—that tomorrow they would be in Monterrey, and this whole stupid, dangerous masquerade would be over. She should never have embarked on it in the first place, she knew, and she could only pray that she would emerge from it relatively unscathed.

Just let me get through tomorrow, she thought, and then it will be all right. I'll be able to take up the rest of my life, and forget this madness. I'll be free.

She kept repeating the word 'free' as if it was a soothing mantra, and eventually it had the effect she wanted and the darkness of night and the shadows of sleep settled on her almost simultaneously.

CHAPTER THREE

It was a maid knocking on the door which woke her eventually. She sat up, pushing her hair back from her face, to find to her horror that it was broad daylight.

'*Señorita*, your car is waiting,' she was reminded, and heard the woman move away.

She glanced at her watch and groaned. She had overslept badly. She dressed rapidly, and almost crammed the loathsome wig on to her hair. She smothered a curse as she adjusted it. She had wanted to meet Ramón in the clear light of day, looking well-groomed and in control of the situation, and instead she was going to appear late, harassed and looking like something the cat had dragged in.

She grabbed her bag and left precipitately, aware that a porter was waiting in the corridor to fetch her cases.

As she emerged from the reception area into the sunshine, she made herself slow down and take deep, steadying breaths, as she saw the waiting car. Lopez was standing beside it, looking anxiously towards the entrance, but when he saw her he smiled in relief and opened the back door.

Nicola, steeling herself, climbed in. But the other seat was unoccupied. She twisted round, looking out of the rear window, but she could only see Lopez supervising the bestowal of her luggage in the boot. When he took his place in the driving seat, she leaned forward.

'Where is Don Ramón?'

He turned. 'I am to give you this, *señorita*.' He handed her an envelope, then closed the glass partition between them.

Nicola opened the envelope and extracted the single sheet it contained.

'I regret that urgent business commitments take me from your side,' the writing, marching arrogantly across the page, informed her. 'I wish you a safe journey, and a pleasant reunion with your *novio*.' It was signed with an unintelligible squiggle.

Nicola read it several times, relief warring with an odd disappointment. So she would never see him again. On the other hand, it meant she only had Lopez to shake off when they reached Monterrey, and that had to be welcome news.

She read the terse words once again, then folded the note and stowed it in her bag, biting her lip.

Later, making sure that Lopez' whole attention was concentrated on the road ahead, she reached into her bag and drew out the itinerary for her trip. There was an airport at Monterrey, and she would have to find out whether there were direct flights from there to Merida. There had been no time to finalise every detail before she left Mexico City. Teresita had seen to it that she had enough money for any eventuality, firmly cutting across her protests.

'You are doing this for my sake, Nicky. It must cost you nothing,' she had said.

In retrospect her words seemed ironic to Nicola now, but she dismissed that trend of thought from her mind, and began reading the brochures for her trip, trying to recapture her earlier excitement at the prospect. But it wasn't easy. The names, the jungle temples no longer seemed to work the same potent magic with her as they had done. Nicola sighed and replaced them in her bag, arranging the crush-proof blue sundress she was going to change into on top of the papers.

She yawned, feeling earlier tensions beginning to seep away. Her little adventure was almost over, and she could begin to relax. Her sleep last night had been fitful, which probably explained her failure to wake this morning. She put her feet up on the seat, and relaxed. Next stop Monterrey, she thought.

It was the car slowing which woke her at last. She struggled to sit upright, putting an apprehensive hand up to touch the wig. She was stiff, and her mouth was dry, as if she had slept for several hours, but surely it couldn't be true.

She expected to see suburbs at least, and signs of an industrial complex, but there wasn't the least indication they were approaching a city. On the contrary, it seemed as if they were in the middle of nowhere. There were vestiges of habitation—a few shacks, and a tin-roofed *cantina*. And the road had altered too. They were no longer on a broad public highway but on a single track dirt road.

There were petrol pumps beside the *cantina* and this was clearly why Lopez was stopping. But where were they?

Lopez came to her door and opened it. 'Do you wish for coffee, *señorita*? I did not wake you for a meal because I thought you would be glad to reach your destination at last.'

'I would be glad of coffee.' She got out of the car. 'When do we reach Monterrey, Lopez? Is this a short-cut?'

The stolid face expressed the nearest thing to amazement it was probably capable of. 'Monterrey, *señorita*? But surely you know—we no longer go to Monterrey. It is Don Luis' order that we should go directly to La Mariposa instead.'

Nicola's lips parted in a soundless gasp. For a moment, she thought she was going to faint, and caught at the edge of the car door to steady herself. She saw Lopez look alarmed, and pretended she had turned her ankle slightly on Teresita's high heels.

She managed to say, 'No—I didn't know.' This must have been the message Ramón had tried to give her, she thought frantically. 'When—when shall we arrive at the *hacienda*?'

'In less than two hours, *señorita*.' He spoke as if expecting to be congratulated. 'You will be pleased, I think, to reach your journey's end.'

Journey's end, Nicola thought as she negotiated with some difficulty the patch of dry and barren ground which separated the *cantina* from the road. Journeys end in lovers' meetings—wasn't that what they said? But there was no lover waiting for her—just a formidable and justly enraged man whose path she had dared to cross.

Inside the *cantina*, a girl was frantically wiping off a table and chairs, and Nicola sank down on to one of them, trying to control her whirling frantic thoughts.

What was she going to do? She knew from Teresita that the Montalba *hacienda* was miles from anywhere, with no nearby stores where she could unobtrusively perform her transformation, or crowded streets for her to fade into. And there was nowhere to hide, or means of escape here. This looked like the kind of place where there might be one bus a week to the nearest town.

The girl brought coffee, black, hot and freshly brewed. Nicola gulped hers. It didn't quench her thirst, but at least helped to revive her a little.

She had been mad to let herself fall asleep again, she reproached herself. If she'd been awake, she would have seen they were turning off the highway, and asked why. She might even have put some kind of a spoke in Don Luis' plans, although it was difficult to know what.

Lopez had come in, and was drinking his coffee at an adjacent table. Moistening her lips, Nicola asked him a little falteringly if he knew why Don Luis had changed his mind about their destination.

'The *Señor* did not honour me with his reasons,' Lopez said a little repressively, then his face relaxed a little. 'But I think, *señorita*, it is because of the chapel. There is a beautiful chapel at La Mariposa and no doubt Don Luis wishes to be married there. It is a family tradition.'

'A family tradition,' Nicola echoed weakly. All

Teresita's forebodings had been right, it seemed. If she had taken this journey in person, there was no way Cliff could ever have traced her. She tried to feel glad for them both, but inwardly her stomach was churning with fright.

She stole a glance at Lopez, wondering what he would do if she threw herself on his mercy and confessed everything. She had money, perhaps she could bribe him to drive her to Monterrey. Then she remembered the note of respect in his voice when he had spoken of Don Luis—the way he had said, '*It is a family tradition*', and knew there was no hope there. He would take her straight to his employer, and a search for Teresita would be mounted immediately. And if by some mischance she and Cliff were still unmarried, then it would all have been for nothing.

She got up abruptly from the table, and asked the girl who had brought the coffee to show her the lavatory which was housed in a rough-and-ready corrugated iron shack across the yard at the rear of the building, where a few scrawny chickens pecked in a desultory manner among the dirt and stones.

The flushing apparatus didn't work, and the tiny handbasin yielded only a trickle of rusty water. Nicola took off her dark glasses and stared at herself in the piece of cracked mirror hanging above the basin. Her eyes looked enormous, and deeply shadowed, and she felt as taut as a bowstring.

It had all gone hopelessly, disastrously wrong, and she had not the faintest idea how to begin to put it right. All she could do, she supposed, was go with the tide, and see where it took her. And if that was to the feet of a furious Mexican grandee, then she had only herself to blame for having got involved in the first place.

As she crossed back to the *cantina*, she noticed a battered blue truck standing in the yard. The driver was standing talking to an older man, probably the *cantina's* owner. Nicola looked longingly at the truck as she passed. She'd asked for a way out of here, and now one was being presented, dangled in front of her, in fact.

But could she take it? The driver had stopped presumably for petrol and a drink, which meant that the truck would be left unattended at some point. But would the driver be obliging enough to leave the keys in the ignition? And how far would she get anyway in a strange vehicle, when only yards away there was a powerful car with a driver who knew the terrain, and would overtake her quite effortlessly because it was his duty to do so?

As she looked away with an inward sigh, she encountered the driver's smiling eyes.

'*Bonita rosita*,' he called, his glance devouring her shamelessly. She saw the *cantina* owner put a hand on his arm, and say something in a low voice. It was obviously some kind of warning, and she heard the word 'Montalba.' The truck driver sobered immediately, his expression becoming almost sheepish, and he turned away shrugging, and moving his hands defensively.

Nicola shivered a little. What kind of man was Don Luis that the mention of his name could have such an instant effect?

On her way back to the table, she saw a telephone booth in the corner. If it hadn't been so totally public and within earshot of anyone who cared to listen, she would have been tempted to try and get through to Mexico City and say to Elaine a loud and unequivocal, 'Help—get me out of here!'

Not that she could blame Elaine for her present predicament, she reminded herself wryly. No one had forced her into this masquerade. She had said herself that it was a crazy idea. She could have and should have stuck to her guns, and refused to have any part in it.

She sat down at the table and drank the rest of her coffee. It was cool now, and left a bitter taste, and she

had to repress a shudder. Lopez had vanished, but
Nicola could hear voices and a giggle emanating from
behind a curtained doorway on the other side of the
bar, and guessed he had taken advantage of her absence
to further his acquaintance with the pretty waitress. His
cap and gloves lay on the table, awaiting his return.
And—Nicola took a shaky breath—so did the keys to
the car. Almost before she knew what she was doing,
she leaned across and took them, dropping them into
her bag. The die was cast, it seemed.

Biting her lip, she got up and crossed to the back
door again. There was no one in sight. The truck basked
in the heat of the afternoon. Nicola looked round, her
heart thudding uncomfortably, then crossed and looked
into the driver's cab. The keys were there, she registered
incredulously. But then why shouldn't they be? This was
a remote corner of nowhere, not a busy urban street.
The door squealed rustily as she opened it, and she froze
for a moment, expecting the sound of running feet,
raised voices, but there was nothing.

She climbed up into the cab, wincing as the heat from
the torn and shabby upholstery penetrated her thin
dress. She drew a deep breath and made herself sit
calmly for a moment while she briefly studied the controls. She needed to make a clean getaway, not fumbling
and stalling. Nor would she take the road they'd just
come on. She would head across country for the distant
sierras, and hope that somewhere she would encounter
the highway or at least a town of reasonable size.

With a silent prayer on her lips, she turned on the
ignition. The engine didn't fire at the first attempt, but
it did at the second, and she eased down the clutch,
swallowing nervously. Bumping and lurching over the
rough ground, the rickety vehicle took off with a speed
which belied its battered exterior.

Behind her, Nicola heard a shout, and then another.
She risked a look over her shoulder. The truck driver
was standing with Lopez, like a frozen tableau depicting

horror, then they both moved, running forward in a futile effort to catch the truck before it was too late. Nicola smiled grimly, and put her foot down hard. A glance in the mirror showed that Lopez had thrown his cap down and was jumping on it, and a giggle of sheer hysteria welled up inside her. She didn't look back again. This was practically desert she was driving over, and she needed all her wits about her.

She drove for over an hour, and then stopped the truck in the shade of a large rock and took stock of her position. So far she hadn't seen as much as a sign of a road, and although she knew she was bound to come across one sooner or later, there was a niggle of anxiety deep in the pit of her stomach. She remembered hearing that drivers were not advised to turn off main roads in the northern regions without qualified guides. Tourists had been known to be lost, and worse. She wasn't a tourist, of course, she was a fugitive, and that made it no better.

There were no maps in the truck, she discovered, after a perfunctory search. There was a service manual for some other vehicle entirely, a dilapidated torch, and a few tools, as well as an oil-stained jacket. No food or drink—not even as much as a slab of chocolate.

Nicola took off the wig and ran her hands luxuriously through her hair. Never again, she thought, and pitched it through the open window. Some desert bird was welcome to use it as a nest. She unzipped her bag and took out the long-suffering blue dress, giving it a critical shake, then found the simple leather sandals she wore with it. When she had changed, she rolled the orchid pink dress and the elegant shoes into a bundle and left them under the rock.

As she re-started the engine, she thought thankfully, 'It's over.'

Another two hours had passed, and Nicola had just realised that she was hopelessly lost, when the truck ran out of fuel. Alerted by the sputtering of the reluctant engine, she searched among the dials on the dashboard for the petrol gauge, and realised with a sinking heart that the needle was vacillating nervously in the red section.

She groaned aloud, wishing that she'd checked more carefully on the fuel situation ages before, although it would have made very little difference. She'd seen no village, filling station, or any other sign of human habitation since she'd embarked on her headlong flight. Plenty of cattle, the odd *burro*, but no people. At first she had been reassured by this, because it also meant no sign of pursuit, but gradually that niggle of anxiety had begun to increase, and now, with the approach of nightfall, anxiety was giving way to fear.

She had no idea where she was. The distant hills seemed no nearer, although that might be some trick of the light, but somehow she didn't think so. She had so constantly had to adapt her route to terrain the truck could cope with that she had begun to suspect she could be driving in a large circle.

The cab had been bakingly hot all afternoon, but now that the sun had set, Nicola knew that it would soon become chilly, and her thin dress would not be adequate protection.

As the truck wheezed to its final stop, she could have burst into tears, but that would solve nothing, she told herself. She had to think. As a stopping place, this was far from ideal. She was in a shallow depression, surrounded by rock and scrub, and it was all too easy to imagine that there were unseen eyes looking down at her.

No more of that, she adjured herself firmly. Positive thinking, my girl, and another more thorough search of the truck. This time she discovered a jerrycan in the back, but it was empty, and she threw it down with a disappointed groan. Under the seat, she came across a couple of lurid girlie magazines which indicated that the truck driver had his own priorities.

She had hoped for a lighter, or at least some matches so she could build a fire. There was enough dry brush around, certainly, but it seemed that the driver didn't include smoking among his vices.

She picked up his jacket and regarded it with disfavour. It was far from clean, but this was no time to fuss about inessentials. Any kind of warmth, however unsavoury, was better than none at all.

She had a long and hungry night ahead of her, and she didn't dare think what the following day would bring, on foot under the blistering sun. She could hardly stay here in this hollow and hope to be found. Even when the inevitable search was mounted, the surrounding rocks would hide her. She tried to think about what she knew of this part of Mexico. It was pitifully little. All her interests had been concentrated on the areas where Aztec and Mayan remains were to be found, yet she could remember one of the men at Trans-Chem talking about a particularly deadly white scorpion which was to be found in the Durango area. Was she anywhere near there? she wondered frantically. And even if not, might there not be other scorpions in various colours it would be wiser to avoid? And mountain lions—she felt certain someone else had mentioned them. Bears too . . .

Oh, stop it, she thought biting her lip. All the same, she wished she had paid slightly more attention to the flora and fauna of this wild country. She'd read somewhere—or had she seen it in a film—that you could keep alive by taking moisture from cactus. But which variety? She'd seen so many. There were others, she knew, which were prized by the Indians for their mind-blowing side effects. That might be the answer, she thought. I could get so high, I'd just float out of here. She chuckled weakly.

It was getting dark very rapidly now, and after only a momentary hesitation she switched on the truck's headlights. Without fuel, there was little point in conserving the battery, and perhaps there was a chance that the lights would be seen, perhaps by a passing aircraft, and investigated. That was a more rational explanation for her action than admitting she was afraid to be alone in the dark, or that if there were wild animals in the vicinity, the lights might keep them at bay.

She picked up the jacket and huddled it round her shoulders with a shiver. Tomorrow, as soon as it dawned, she would set off towards the east again, and see how far she could get before finding some shelter against the fierce heat of the day.

But now she needed to rest. The next day was going to take as much energy as she possessed. She curled up on the seat, her cheek resting on her hand like a child's. Sleep came more easily than she could have hoped, worn out as she was by the tensions of the past few days and the long struggle with an unfamiliar and often recalcitrant vehicle. She dreamed of Barton Abbas and her childhood, lying in a cornfield and watching a hawk turn in a long slow circle in the blue sky above her. It was peaceful and reassuring, and Nicola's lips curved contentedly as she slept. It was good to be a child again, to let the worries and pressures of adult life slide away. Good to be in a sunlit landscape and watch the hovering hawk—until suddenly the dream tilted sideways into nightmare, where the hawk was swooping, and she was the prey, transfixed and helpless, unable to run or defend herself.

She sat up with a little cry, staring round her. The air in the cab was chill, but she was drenched with sweat, and shaking. What had woken her? she wondered dazedly. The dream—or something else? Some sound?

She reached for the torch and slid across the seat to the door. She climbed down from the cab slowly and gingerly and stood rigidly, her head bent, listening.

Yes, there was a sound. A chinking, scraping sound. She shrank nearer to the bulk of the truck, gripping the torch, and peering into the pool of light still cast by the headlights. The torch was hardly ideal for the function it had been designed for, but it was all she had as a weapon.

Hooves, she thought, still listening intently, her nerves screwed up to screaming point. More cattle? Another burro?

There was a shadow now on the edge of the circle of light, a big dense shadow which moved, and she heard the unmistakable creak of harness, and a soft whinny.

She called out, '*Quien es?*'

The shadow moved forward into the light. Dark horse, dark rider. A man, dressed in black, with a broad-brimmed hat shadowing his face. Her hand tightened round the torch.

He said, '*Que pasa?*'

Her body went rigid. Those two laconic syllables had been delivered in a voice which was only too familiar. But it couldn't be true, she argued desperately with herself. Ramón was miles away on his cousin's business. He couldn't be here. Surely fate couldn't play her a trick like that. It was her own nervousness, the fact that she'd just woken up from a bad dream that was making her imagine that it was no one but him confronting her from the back of the tall black gelding.

Almost dizzily she waited for his accusation, and then realisation dawned. He didn't recognise her. How could he? When he'd seen her, she'd been a vivid brunette dressed in pink, speaking Spanish—whereas now . . .

She said slowly and haltingly with no accent at all, '*Señor—me he perdida.*'

'So you are lost,' he said in English. 'It is hardly surprising. This is not good country to drive in. There is a good road ten kilometres to the south. Why didn't you use that?'

She hesitated. 'I was heading that way—but the truck ran out of fuel.'

'Would it not have been wise to have filled up the tank before starting on your journey?'

'I—I left in rather a hurry,' she said, her heart beating so loudly it seemed impossible that he shouldn't hear it. 'I—I'm also very hungry and thirsty.'

He nodded. 'No gasoline, no food and drink and——' he looked her over—'no adequate clothing. Even for a crazy *turista*, you seem singularly badly equipped. Where did you get the truck?'

His tone was hardly sympathetic, but the abruptness of the final question threw her. It would be just her luck if he recognised the damned thing. She would have to be careful.

She said, 'That's a little difficult to explain, *señor*.'

'Try.' It was a command, not an invitation.

'I—I needed a lift, and the truck was going in the right direction—only the driver—misunderstood.'

'I think the misunderstanding was yours, *señorita*. You are even crazier than I thought, to have accepted such a favour from a stranger.'

'It wasn't a favour,' she protested. 'I was going to pay. I have money.'

'But not the currency he wanted, plainly.' For the first time, he sounded amused. 'And may I ask the fate of this man?'

'He—he got out of the truck—to relieve himself. I drove away and left him,' she improvised wildly.

'You are truly resourceful, *señorita*,' he drawled. 'I will bid you *adios*. No one with wit as keen, or so strong a sense of self-preservation, can possibly be in need of my poor assistance.'

His hand went up to his hat brim in a mocking salute, and he turned the horse's head.

My God, Nicola thought, he's going! She ran forward.

'*Señor*—please! You—you can't just leave me here like this!'

Her movement startled the horse. It threw up its head

and began to sidestep, only to be brought effortlessly back under control by its rider.

He said coolly, 'I have told you where the road is, *señorita*. To walk that distance should not be beyond your powers. You seem young and healthy.'

Nicola stared up at him, wondering how on earth she had ever found him attractive. His face was dark and forbidding under the shadow of his hat, his mouth harsh and uncompromising.

She hated him more than she had ever dreamed it was possible to hate anyone, but she made her voice pleading. 'I'm tired, and hungry—and very frightened, *señor*. There must be some shelter of some kind that you know of.' She paused, and then said flatly, 'I'll pay you to take me there!'

'Aren't you afraid I might ask the same price as the truck driver? You wouldn't rid yourself of me quite so easily.'

Nicola swallowed. 'That's a chance I shall have to take. I—I don't want to spend the night alone in that truck.'

'I think you already take too many chances, *señorita*.' His tone was soft and chilling.

Nicola shivered inside the jacket. This was a side of Ramón she had not seen before. No sign now of the charm, or the sensual teasing which had so embarrassed and disturbed her.

Her hands gripped together. She said in a low voice, 'Please help me.'

There was a silence, then he shrugged slightly. 'Very well. Tonight we will find some shelter, and in the morning we will see what is best to be done. Are you travelling quite alone?'

'No,' she said hastily. 'I'm joining friends. In Monterrey. That's where I was heading for.'

'Then you are well off the track, *señorita*.' Again that faint amusement. 'At the moment you are on your way to La Mariposa, the hacienda of Don Luis Alvarado de Montalba. You have perhaps heard of him?'

She forced herself to say casually, 'I think I've heard the name—yes. Is this his land?'

'It is. And he would be desolated to know that he was harbouring unsuspected so charming a guest. Perhaps I should take you to the *hacienda*.'

'No.' She hoped he hadn't picked up that note of panic. She tried to laugh. 'Please, *señor*, I'm not really in any fit state to meet any great Spanish landowner. I've behaved like a complete fool, and I know it. If you could just guide me to where I can get transport for Monterrey, I'd be eternally grateful, but I don't want to meet this Don Luis.'

'Very well,' he said evenly. 'What luggage have you?'

'Just a bag.'

'Then I suggest you fetch it, so that we can be off.'

She was pulling it out of the truck when the thought struck her that if nothing else he might recognise the bag. But she could hardly pretend that she had lost it, and there must be a million similar bags in the world, she told herself, slinging it over her shoulder like a satchel. If the worst came to the worst, she would brazen it out.

But he never gave it a second glance. 'The horse has good manners. You need not be frightened.'

I wish I could say the same for his owner, Nicola thought as she unwillingly prepared to accept his assistance. She'd expected the use of a stirrup and perhaps a helping hand into the saddle, but instead he bent towards her, his arm going round her waist and lifting her as if she was a featherweight. And she was to sit in front of him, she discovered to her dismay.

She ventured on a protest. 'I know how to ride, *señor*.'

'I have already commented on your resourcefulness, *señorita*. Unlike the unhappy driver of the truck, I prefer to keep you where I can see you. And I should warn you that Malagueno accepts you on his back because I

am here, but you should make no attempt to ride him
alone.'

Nicola stared straight in front of her, glad that he
could not read her expression. Her paramount wish was
that she had pushed jeans instead of a dress into her
bag, although the skirt was full enough to allow her to
ride astride without too much difficulty. But it still
revealed more of her slender legs than she could have
wished under the circumstances, and this made her feel
nervous and vulnerable and acutely conscious of her
femininity. But then that was how she had been feeling
from the moment she had met him, she thought in self-
accusation.

'Relax, *señorita*.' His voice was mocking. 'I am told
that rape on horseback is not merely dangerous but
impossible, so you need have no fears.'

She didn't deign to answer, but instead caught hold
of the edge of the saddle to steady herself, while gripping
a handful of Malagueno's mane with the other hand.

She was held in the circle of his arms, but casually.
He made no attempt to hold her more intimately, and
she was thankful, because she was finding their present
proximity, the warmth of his breath on her neck and
ear quite disturbing enough. The truck seemed suddenly
a much safer bet, but she could hardly say at this stage
that she had changed her mind.

A weird inhuman sound broke the stillness of the
night air, and she shuddered, tightening her fingers in
Malagueno's mane. 'What was that?'

'A coyote,' he said. 'Or did you think they existed
only in movies?'

That settled it. The truck would stay where it was,
unattended, although she would have to make arrangements of some kind for its recovery in Monterrey. But
what, she couldn't even begin to think.

All she could in fact think about was the strange
workings of fate which had brought Ramón back into
her life when she had been sure she would never see him

again. In fact, she'd counted on it. His dark and dangerous attraction had roused feelings and emotions in her which she wanted no part of. And if some foresight could have warned her that she would be spending the night in his company, even if it was on horseback, then she would never have embarked on her flight in the first place. It would have been preferable to have allowed Lopez to convey her to La Mariposa and the wrath of Don Luis, she thought. She stifled a little sigh, and looked up at the dark velvet of the sky with its spangling of stars.

'No moon,' she commented, half to herself.

'Alas, no. Nor a balcony, nor a *mariachi* band.' The mockery was open now, and she scowled, remembering that moment in the restaurant when he had sent the musicians away.

'It was just a remark,' she said, glad that the darkness hid the sudden colour in her cheeks.

'And the sigh?'

Was there a trick he didn't miss? she wondered.

'Let's just say I've had a bad day and leave it at that.' She paused. 'Malagueno's a beautiful horse—very sure-footed.'

'He suits me very well,' he said laconically. 'He bears his name because his sire came from Malaga.'

Another silence. She hastened to fill it with words. 'You said that all this was Montalba land. It must be a vast estate.'

'It was once. Now much of it belongs to the *ejidatarios*, peasants who are given free grants of land by the government. Here in the north much land which was once pasture for cattle is now being turned into small farms.'

'You don't agree with government policy?'

'All men must live,' he said after a pause. 'And the Montalbas could well spare the land. Some of the *ejidatarios* work hard on their holdings, but others do not. They find the life too hard, and prefer to remain peasants, selling their labour as they can.'

'As you do yours?' Nicola asked slyly.

'As I do mine,' he agreed.

She was disconcerted. She had expected at this point that he would tell her that he was Ramón de Costanza, cousin of the great Don Luis. She could see no point in his keeping it a secret. The thought that perhaps he was not communicating his identity because she was not of sufficient importance was a riling one.

Meanwhile this ride through the darkness was playing havoc with her unaccustomed muscles, and she moved restlessly.

'Is it much further—wherever we're going?'

There was a smile in his voice. 'I thought you were used to horses, *chica*. But no, you will not have to suffer for much longer.'

'Where are we going?'

'So many questions.' He sounded faintly exasperated. 'We are going to a nearby *ejido*.'

Nicola's spirits rose slightly. It sounded hopeful. A house, however primitive, occupied by a farmer and possibly his wife and family too. Food and warmth, and somewhere to lay her head. But most of all, other people, she thought with sudden unease.

She began to peer forward into the darkness, looking for a lighted window, but there was only the night, which made it all the more surprising when her companion said, 'Your ordeal is over, *señorita*. We have arrived at our destination.'

Malagueno had stopped, and lowered his head to crop at unseen grass. Nicola found she was being lowered to the ground beside him, and she ran her fingers caressingly down the satiny neck. '*Gracias*, Malagueno,' she said under her breath.

Dismounting, her companion looped the horse's reins over the branch of a nearby tree.

'Where is this place?' She stared round her helplessly.

'You don't believe it exists?' His hand closed round

her arm, and she was urged gently but firmly forward. Had she been alone, she could well have blundered into it, she realised. It was only a shape, slightly darker and more solid than the darkness around it. No lights, no dogs barking, or friendly welcome of any kind. In fact it looked—deserted.

She said sharply, 'Where is everyone?'

'There is no one but ourselves,' he said coolly. 'Believe me, *chica*, when you see the size of the cabin, you will be grateful.'

Nicola felt anything but grateful. She hung back as he opened the door, which creaked eerily.

'Frightened?' He was laughing at her again. 'Wait here, then, while I light a lamp, and dislodge any intruders which may have taken up residence in Miguel's absence.'

'There's no need for that,' Nicola protested. 'Other people are just as entitled to a night's shelter and . . .'

'I was not thinking of people,' he said gently, and a shudder went through her, as she suddenly imagined unnamed horrors waiting there in the dark. Rats, she thought. Ugh—or scorpions—or even—snakes.

She heard the rasp of a match and saw a glimmer of light which gradually swelled into a steady flame. A moment later, and another appeared in a corner of the room. Nicola stepped gingerly across the threshold and looked around her. It was not a prepossessing sight which met her eyes. There was a blackened fireplace built into one wall, with a rusty-looking cooking pot suspended from a hook in the chimney, and in the opposite wall was a deep alcove with a wooden bedstead actually built into it. A frayed curtain hung from a rough pole above the alcove, and could be drawn for privacy, Nicola supposed. The first lamp her companion had lit hung from the ceiling. The second stood on a square wooden table in the corner. Two stools and a lumpy mattress on the bed seemed to supply the rest of the furnishings.

Something of her feelings must have shown on her face, because her companion gave a low laugh. 'What did you expect, Señorita Turista? A room at the Continental in Mexico City?'

She looked at him, her eyes widening involuntarily. He had discarded his hat and the poncho-like garment he had been wearing during the ride. The elegant urban suit had gone too, and he was wearing close fitting dark pants and superbly made riding boots. Another of those expensive dark-coloured silk shirts moulded his shoulders and chest. He looked the business man no longer, but very much the man of action, and Nicola realised suddenly that in this guise he was even more formidable. She felt the force of his attraction before, but now she had no charade to hide behind, no outraged grandee's *novia* to play. She was herself alone, and she realised with alarm that he was watching her in that same speculative way as at their first meeting, as if he was both amused and intrigued.

For a moment their eyes held in silent challenge, then he gave a slight shrug and turned away.

He said, 'I'll get a fire started. There's some food in my saddle bag. Perhaps you would get us a meal while I attend to Malagueno.'

Again she rushed into speech. 'Where did you learn to speak such good English?'

'Here and there. Where I could.'

She said, 'You're not very communicative.' She forced a laugh. 'Have you got something to hide?'

'No, *chica*,' he said softly. 'Have you?'

He disappeared through a door at the back of the cabin, leaving her gasping. When he returned he was carrying a bundle of firewood which he arranged deftly in the fireplace, and coaxed into flame with his matches.

'You certainly know how to make yourself at home,' Nicola commented, recovering a little. 'You mentioned Miguel. Does he own this place, and is he a friend of yours?'

'He did, and he was.' He stood up dusting his hands together.

'He's dead. I—I'm sorry.'

He shook his head. 'Miguel is very much alive. I'll go and get that food.'

Nicola sat down on one of the stools and stretched her legs out in front of her. There was no real warmth from the fire yet, but the flicker of the flames was in itself a comfort. And comfort was what she needed, because her unease was deepening with every moment that passed.

Ramón had changed, and not just in exterior details like his clothes. His manner had changed too. It was cooler and more incisive. On the journey at times he had seemed a charming playboy, but there was no trace of that any more. Now, he was no one's second in command. He behaved like a man who was used to giving orders and having them obeyed.

She thought, 'But of course he runs the ranch, and he's back on his own territory. That explains it.'

But her explanation lacked conviction, and she knew it. There was something deeply wrong, something which was eluding her.

'*Que pasa?*' She started violently and turned to find him watching her from the doorway, frowning. 'You are very pale. Are you ill?'

Nicola shook her head. 'Reaction, I suppose.' She tried a weak laugh. 'It's been quite a day.'

And could turn out to be quite a night too. She had tried to avoid looking at the bed in the alcove. Even with the curtain drawn, it was far from being a sanctuary.

With an effort she turned to the articles he had just placed on the table—a can of some kind of stew, with an opener, a packet of coffee, and a tin mug and plate.

He met her gaze, and the corner of his mouth lifted in a sardonic smile. 'I regret there are no tortillas. I apologise too that there is only one set of dishes.'

That, she assured him silently, doesn't worry me half as much as the fact that there's only one bed.

'There is a well in the yard at the rear.' He pointed to another door at the back of the cabin. 'I'll fetch you some water. There is also a hut there—for your convenience.'

'Thank you,' Nicola muttered, and he laughed.

'The word is '*gracias*,' he said. 'Perhaps after we have eaten I will give you a lesson in Spanish. You can hardly hope to traverse my country on the two phrases you have used so far.'

'No,' she said weakly. She had pushed her leather bag under the table hoping it would be less obtrusive there, and she saw him look at it as he turned to leave, but he said nothing and she breathed again. She debated whether or not to take off the truck driver's jacket and decided against it. In one pocket, her fingers encountered the torch which she had completely forgotten about, and its solid presence idiotically cheered her.

There was a sink in one corner of the room, consisting of a tin bowl with an attached waste pipe. Nicola decided that one priority was to give the cooking pot even a rudimentary wash. There was an enamel coffee pot, battered but usable, standing under the sink, and Nicola shook her head as she looked at it. The preparation of this meal was going to be a challenge, and surviving it could well be a miracle.

Yet, in the event, it proved simpler than she had imagined, and when the spicy savoury smell of the stew began to fill the cabin, Nicola forgot her qualms and allowed herself to realise how hungry she was.

She knew he was watching her. They were watching each other, taking each other's measure like adversaries who know battle is about to begin. She'd seen him bring in a blanket roll and toss it on to the bed, and had bent towards her cooking, glad that the heat from the fire gave her an excuse for the sudden flare of colour in her face.

She tried to remind herself of all the times she had been alone with Ewan. When she had been close in his arms, kissed and caressed by him as he tried to persuade her to let him make love to her. Yet even then she had always felt she was ultimately in control of the situation.

But not with this man, she thought. This man who was a law unto himself.

He came back into the cabin, humming softly to himself. She recognised the tune. It was the one the *mariachi* band had been playing at the hotel restaurant, and her face went blank as she listened.

'Is the food ready?' he broke off the tune to ask, and she jumped.

'Er—yes, but I don't know how we're going to manage ...'

'I found a fork and spoon in my saddlebag. You can have the spoon.'

Her hands were shaking as she tried to ladle the stew on to the plate, but eventually she managed and placed it on the table between them. She picked up the spoon and made herself eat, forcing each mouthful down her reluctant throat, while her mind ran feverishly like a tiny animal on a wheel.

His choice of tune had been purely fortuitous, she tried to reassure herself. He hadn't recognised her. To him, she was just a silly tourist who'd got herself into a difficult situation and wanted to be rescued.

'You are very quiet.' He was watching her. 'Have you run out of questions, *chica*?'

All, except for the sixty-four-thousand-dollar one, she thought shakily, and I don't think I want to know the answer to that.

She tried to smile. 'Tell me some more about Miguel.'

He shrugged. 'He was a friend, and the son of a friend. While he was at university, he became imbued with political ideals about equality. He saw it as his duty to work with the *ejiditarios*, and fight for their rights. He even tried to become one of them—not with any great success, as you see.'

'And you disagreed with him?'

'No. I respected his view, his ideals. But then the government's measures on land reform were not sufficient for him. They did not move fast enough. He began to say that landowners who were unwilling to surrender their estates should be dispossessed—by force if necessary. And he did not stop at talking. He led a group of *peons* to an estate north of here. They had guns, shots were fired, and an overseer injured. Miguel has placed himself outside the law.'

Nicola asked huskily, 'What happened? Did the landowner agree to their demands, and give up his land?'

'*Si*.' His mouth curled. 'The spineless fool.'

Her heart missed a beat. 'You wouldn't do so?'

'No,' he said softly. His eyes met hers across the table, as hard as obsidian. 'What I give, I give, but I allow nothing to be taken from me against my will.'

She went on looking at him, trying to tell herself she had imagined that note of menace in his voice.

He said, 'You appear nervous, *chica*. Are you?'

'No,' she denied too hastily.

'Don't lie to me. I can see fear in your eyes. I told you once how much you can learn from a woman's eyes. I am glad that you have taken off your glasses at last, Señorita Tarrant.'

Her throat seemed to close with fright. She said, 'How—how do you know my name?'

'You still wish to play games?' He shrugged. 'While you were asleep that first day I looked in your bag and found your passport. I had to know, you see, who was masquerading as Teresita Dominguez.'

'But how did you know?' Nicola said huskily. 'You haven't seen Teresita since she was a child.'

He shook his head. 'Wrong, *señorita*. You see, I have also been playing a game with you. It is my cousin Ramón who is a stranger to Teresita. I know her well.'

Nicola had a weird sensation that the cabin walls were closing in on her. She pushed the stool back so violently that it fell with a clatter, and stood up.

She said, 'Who are you?'

He rose too. He seemed to tower over her. 'I, *señorita*? As I am sure you have guessed already, I am Luis Alvarado de Montalba.'

She heard herself gasp, saw the barely controlled anger in the dark face, the glitter in his eyes, and saw his hands curving like talons as he reached for her. She remembered the hawk plunging on its prey out of the clear sky, and cried out as she too plunged into swirling darkness.

CHAPTER FOUR

CONSCIOUSNESS returned slowly. Nicola was aware of a feeling of nausea and oppression, and then a cup placed at her lips. She was told succinctly, 'Drink,' and liquid like fire trickled into her mouth and down her throat. She moaned faintly and moved her head from side to side, trying to escape, but the arm which held her was implacable, and she was incapable, anyway, of any real resistance.

Eventually she opened her eyes. She was lying on the bed in the alcove, which explained the sense of oppression. She turned her head warily and surveyed the rest of the cabin. The lamp on the table had been turned low, and this, with the firelight, provided the only illumination.

He was there, her captor, her enemy, sitting beside the fireplace, staring into the flames. Then, as if aware that she had stirred, he turned and looked at her.

Nicola made as if to sit up and realised just in time that her blue dress was lying across the foot of the bed, and that her only covering was her lacy half-cup bra and tiny briefs. She snatched at the blanket and wrapped it around herself quickly, then realised what a fool she was being. There was only one person who could have removed her dress, so what use was there in trying to conceal herself from him? He could already have looked his fill while she was unconscious, she thought, shamed to her bones.

Something else she noticed too. Her bag had been emptied and her money, tickets and passport stood in forlorn heaps on the table.

Luis Alvarado de Montalba rose from his stool and walked across the room. Nicola turned her head away

and closed her eyes to block out the sight of him.
Unbidden, a tear squeezed out from beneath her lashes
and trickled down the curve of her cheek.

'Weeping, *chica*?' he mocked. 'What for? Your past
sins, or their future retribution?'

She said in a low voice, 'I can explain.'

'I am sure you can,' he said drily. 'I am sure your
fertile imagination can probably conjure up at least a
dozen explanations, but this time I want the truth.
Where is Teresita Dominguez?'

'Safe from you by this time, I hope,' she said wearily.

'You speak as if I pose some threat to Teresita,' he
remarked.

'Don't you?' Her voice was bitter. 'I suppose an ego
like yours can only imagine that a proposal of marriage
from you would flatter and overwhelm any woman. It
would never occur to you that Teresita would find the
prospect of marrying you utterly repulsive.'

'You speak as if I planned to drag her to the altar by
her hair.' The dark eyes glinted as he looked down at
her. 'I promise that I had no such intention. I believed
that she was as—resigned to the idea of our marriage as
myself.' He paused. 'But I had not allowed for the influ-
ences which would be brought to bear on her once she
had left the convent.'

Nicola gasped. 'Then—you knew about that?'

'Naturally I knew,' he returned impatiently. 'She was
my ward, therefore it was my business to know when
she left the shelter of the accommodation I had provided
for her. However, I was assured by the general manager
of Trans-Chem that you and the other girl were respect-
able, and that Teresita would only benefit from your
company. How wrong he was!'

'Then you also knew we'd met Teresita at Trans-
Chem?' Nicola sank back on the mattress, utterly chag-
rined.

'Of course. I arranged for her to work there on a
temporary basis at one time, because she was insistent

that she wished to have a job like other girls.' A wintry smile touched the corners of his mouth. 'I imagine you know how that worked out. She was given the job as a favour to me because I was on the board of the company for which Trans-Chem were acting as consultants. I imagine it was only out of respect for me that she was not ignominiously sacked on the first day.'

'How well informed you are,' Nicola said bitterly. 'It was lucky for Teresita that your informant slipped up over Cliff.'

'If you refer to Clifford Arnold, I knew about his visits from the beginning, but I did not take them seriously.' His mouth twisted cynically. 'I did not grudge the child a flirtation. Knowing her, I was sure it would go no further than that.'

'Then you're wrong.' Nicola lifted her chin defiantly. 'Cliff is Teresita's husband by now.'

'I would not be too sure of that,' he said coolly. 'There are lengthy formalities before any marriage can take place between a Mexican national and a foreigner.'

She heard him with dismay. The legal aspect of the situation had not really occurred to her. She'd heard so much about the ease of divorce and marriage in Mexico that she had not realised there could be any snags where the bridal couple were of mixed nationalities.

So it had all been for nothing, she thought miserably, and a little sob escaped her.

'Don't think you will escape the penalties of your actions by such abject behaviour,' he said crushingly. 'What happened to the spirit you showed over the past two days?'

'I'm not crying for myself,' she choked, 'but for Teresita.'

'Then I would save your tears,' he said caustically. 'She seems in little need of them.'

'No?' She stared up at him accusingly. 'When you're going to go to Mexico City, and drag her away from the man she loves? When you're going to ruin her life?'

He shrugged. 'Teresita has taken her future into her own hands. Whether or not her life is ruined would seem to depend on herself and this man she has chosen. However, she is of age, so legally no concern of mine. I shall not interfere.'

Nicola digested this in some bewilderment. 'But don't you even care?'

'Oh yes, *chica*,' he said silkily. 'I care that I have been made a fool of. I care that Teresita allowed the arrangements for our marriage to go ahead without informing me that she no longer wished to become my wife. I care that a stranger has forced her way into my life, throwing my plans into chaos.'

'But what does that matter? You never really wanted Teresita. You can't have done!'

'The match was made between our families,' he said bleakly. 'Perhaps neither of us was overjoyed at the prospect, but we could have expected to be reasonably happy—eventually. It is time I was married. I have a number of houses, but no real home. I need a son to whom I can pass on the inheritance I have built for him. I need some grace and serenity in my life. I felt Teresita could give me these things.'

Nicola's eyes flashed. 'It sounds a very one-sided bargain to me. What would Teresita be getting in return for bearing your children and surrounding you with 'grace and serenity'? The sort of joyless, loveless relationship which your family has specialised in probably for generations?'

His mouth curled. 'You will not speak of my family in that way, *señorita*. Your tongue will be your downfall.'

'Don't you like to hear the truth?'

His hands descended on her shoulders, jerking her into a sitting position.

'And what do you know of truth?' he said harshly. 'You—who have acted a lie since the moment I saw you. What do you know of love? You talk a great deal, *chica*, but your eyes tell me that you are as untutored in passion as Teresita herself.'

His words were like a lash across an open wound.

'That isn't true,' she cried in protest. 'I've been in love—deeply and passionately in love. I love him still. That's why I decided to help Teresita to be happy. Because I knew that she deserved better than the pallid, cold-blooded arrangement which was all you were offering.'

His smile was grim. 'So you think me cold-blooded, *amiga*? I promise that Teresita would not have found me so. And neither will you.'

He pulled her towards him, and his mouth descended mercilessly on hers. She was unable to breathe or even think coherently. Panic rose in her, and she beat with clenched fists on his shoulders, but neither his hold nor his brutal assault on the softness of her lips slackened even for a moment. Her half-covered breasts were crushed achingly against the muscular wall of his chest, and a whimper rose in her throat as his hand twisted in her tangled hair, dragging her head back, so that his mouth could travel bruisingly down the length of her throat.

When she could speak, she said pleadingly, 'No—please!'

He lifted his head and stared down at her, his eyes glittering with mockery, and something else that she was frightened to interpret.

'Who is speaking now, *chica*? The experienced woman of the world in your imagination, or the frightened virgin of reality? I want the truth!'

Her throat closed, making speech impossible. She could only shake her head, staring up at him with eyes that begged wordlessly for understanding, even for mercy.

Almost gently, he lowered her back on to the mattress. Then he sat up, his eyes travelling slowly and broodingly down the slender length of her body. Nicola felt humiliated under the intensity of his gaze, but she made no effort to drag the blanket around her, or even shield herself with her hands. She deserved to feel this shame, she thought, just as she deserved every harsh word he had thrown at her, and more. Whatever her private opinion of his motives or morals, she'd had no right to interfere. He was entitled to be angry, even to exact some kind of retribution, but not—in that way. Dear God, not that.

His hand cupped her chin, forcing her to look up at him, and one finger stroked softly and sensuously across the swollen outline of her mouth.

He said very quietly, 'You have done me a great wrong, *amiga*. You have insulted me, and robbed me, and made me lose face. Are you prepared to make amends?'

'If I can.' She tried to sound brave, but in spite of her efforts there was a quiver in her voice.

'Oh, you can,' he said softly. 'I need a wife, as I told you. Thanks to you, the girl I had chosen is lost to me. The least you can do is take her place.'

For a moment she lay staring up at him, her mind trying to make sense of what he had just said. She began to shake her head slowly.

'No, you can't—I couldn't! You're not serious.'

'No?' he asked mockingly. 'Perhaps another display of my ardour will convince you.' He bent towards her, and her hands came up, pushing against him.

'No!' Her voice cracked in panic, and he laughed.

'Then say you will marry me, and I will wait like a gentleman until you are legally mine.'

'But you don't want to marry me. You can't want to. We don't know each other. You don't like me . . .' The words tumbled over each other. She knew she wasn't making any sense, but then what was in this whole crazy situation?

'You have made me very angry, I admit,' he said. 'But you inspire other emotions in me, *amiga*, which

make fair recompense for any amount of anger. Why
do you imagine I did not unmask you immediately? Why
did I allow you to think I was Ramón? Because you
intrigued me, *chica*. Because you stirred my blood.
My decision to escort Teresita north myself was a
last-minute one, prompted by a sense of duty.' His
mouth twisted ruefully. 'I felt I owed it to the
child—and myself—to spend some time with her, to get
to know her—perhaps, if she seemed willing, to woo
her.'

'How kind of you,' said Nicola on a little flare of
bitterness. 'I'm sure she would have been overwhelmed.'

'You flatter me, *chica*,' he said mockingly.

But in a moment of self-revelation, she knew that
wasn't the case. He was a practised seducer. If he had
employed the same wiles with Teresita as he had with
her, she would have been eating out of his hand by the
time they reached La Mariposa. She remembered with
shame her own reactions. And she knew without looking
at him that he was remembering too.

After a pause, he said, 'But I must confess, I wasn't
looking forward to the journey, until the car stopped
outside the convent and I saw you waiting for me, *chica*.
For a moment I was not even sure what was happening,
and then you spoke and I realised that it was all a trick
to fool my unfortunate cousin. The impulse to turn the
tables on you was irresistible.'

She shook her head. 'But—weren't you worried about
Teresita—that she might have been harmed in some
way?'

'If it was that, there would have been a ransom note
waiting, not a girl in disguise. No, I guessed at once
that you were one of the girls with whom she was sharing an apartment, and that you were the English girl,
because I knew the American spoke little Spanish. Yours
is excellent. I must congratulate you.'

Nicola swallowed. 'But why did you let it—go on like
that?'

'Because I was bored. I decided that you might alleviate that boredom, provide me with some amusement on the trip. Which you did, *amiga*,' he added cynically. 'Although only by day, to my regret. I had not envisaged that I would be spending my nights alone, but then it had not occurred to me that a girl who could lend herself to such an adventure could possibly be as innocent as you were.'

His eyes met hers, and she felt a shock run through her entire body. 'I want you, Nicola, and I intend to have you—with the bonds of matrimony or without them. The choice is yours.'

'And if I say I won't marry you?'

He gave a slight shrug. 'Then instead of La Mariposa, we'll go somewhere else. To my house near Acapulco, perhaps. At night, the bedroom is full of the sound of the ocean.'

'Fascinating,' she said, conscious that her heart was beating wildly. 'I'm sure that all your lady loves find that a terrific turn-on. Only I won't be joining them. Isn't there any other choice beside the two you've mentioned?'

'Oh yes. There is the little matter of the stolen truck. We still operate the Napoleonic code in Mexico, *querida*. You would have to prove your innocence of the theft. Our jails are not comfortable places, as you would have a long time to find out. On the other hand, the truck could be retrieved, and the driver handsomely compensated for the trouble and inconvenience you have caused him. I could probably persuade him to bring no charges against you—or I could wash my hands of the whole affair and allow justice to take its course with you.'

Dry-mouthed, she protested, 'But I didn't steal it! I—I only borrowed it. I was going to let the driver know where I'd left it and ...'

'How?' he said unanswerably.

There was a long silence, then Nicola said huskily,

'But—your family. What will they say? They know you intended to marry Teresita.'

'*Si*,' he agreed. 'There was a small sensation earlier today when I informed them that I had changed my plans. My aunt was overjoyed, taking it as a sign that I am about to gratify her by proposing to my cousin Pilar.' His mouth twisted. 'But I am not. I therefore blighted her hopes yet again by requesting her to have a room prepared for you. It was not long afterwards that I received an agitated phone call from Lopez.'

'Oh,' she said guiltily.

'Oh, indeed, *chica*,' he agreed rather grimly. 'I still do not understand how he can have been such a fool, especially after I had warned him to be vigilant. The tickets and itinerary in your bag made your intentions perfectly clear.'

She bit her lip. 'But you've told your family about me. And about me running away?'

'Some of it,' he said. 'Not the whole story.'

She spread her hands. 'Then you must see how impossible it is. They would never accept me as—as a suitable wife for you.'

He lifted a cynical shoulder. 'Tia Isabella would never accept any woman I chose, but you needn't fear her, or any of them. Only Lopez and my cousin Ramón know of the deception that you attempted to practise. And it will never be referred to again by anyone if I make it known that is my wish.'

'How nice to have such power over people,' Nicola said bitterly. 'But don't expect it to work with me. I hate and despise you and all you stand for, and I always shall. Do you really want to be married to a woman who finds you—repugnant?'

'No, and I might hesitate if I thought that it was true. But I don't believe you, Nicola.' His hand smoothed her bare shoulder, then slid down to the curve of her breast where it swelled above the lacy confine of her bra. Nicola felt her breathing thicken uncontrollably and a spasm of sensation clench in her body, so exquisitely intense that she could have cried out, as his fingers pushed the lace aside and circled the throbbing rosy peak. He looked down at her, the dark face taut, its planes and angles suddenly sharply accentuated. 'Deny it now,' he said hoarsely. 'Deny that I can make you want me—if you dare.'

She didn't dare. Huskily she said, 'Please—stop.'

'Then promise me that you will marry me.' His fingers still moved on her, creating their own delicious agony. 'Promise me—before I finish what I began with your dress, and take you here and now.'

Her hands dug into the mattress as she had to fight to stop her body arching towards him in mute and helpless invitation. She whispered, 'Yes, I'll marry you—only—no more, please.'

For a moment he remained very still, then, with a faint groan, he pushed himself away from her and drew up the blanket to cover her body.

'You spoke only just in time, *querida*,' he said unevenly. '*Dios*, Nicola, fight me all you wish in the day, but at night, in my arms, you will do what I want—be what I want.'

Nicola said nothing. Her eyes closed, and she turned her head away, trying to hide the dull, hot colour which had invaded her face. She wanted to die of shame—shame at the ease of her capitulation—shame because of the wild aching excitement he had so easily roused in her. For over a year she had worn her Snow Queen image like invisible armour, yet all the defences which hurt and disillusion had built round her had vanished like thistledown in the wind as soon as he had touched her. And even before that, she thought, lashing herself as she remembered her body's helpless arousal in the car the previous day.

And if she had responded then, accepted his insolent invitation? Well, she would belong to him—would be on her way with him to the villa near Acapulco or some other suitable love nest for a few weeks, or perhaps even months.

Not that marriage would really change anything, she made herself realise. It would only bring more hurt, more disillusionment eventually. Because it couldn't work. Once his frankly expressed desire for her body was sated, there would be nothing left.

She would live at La Mariposa, or one of his other houses, and bring up his children, and try not to wonder where he was when the bed beside her remained empty. It was the sort of existence she had pityingly envisaged for Teresita—that was why she was here—but not for herself. Never for herself.

She heard Luis moving round the room, and opened her eyes a little. He was raking down the fire, and the lamp on the table was already out. As she watched, he stood up and came back to the alcove. He sat down on the edge of the bed and started to pull his boots off.

She said, 'What are you doing?'

'Preparing for bed,' he said briefly. 'It is time we got some sleep.' He glanced at her and grinned when he saw the all too evident apprehension on her face. 'Don't alarm yourself, *querida*. My boots are all I intend to remove—unless you insist, of course,' he added mockingly.

She moistened dry lips. 'You promised . . .'

'And I shall keep my word.' He swung himself fully on to the bed beside her. 'However, I do not intend to spend what remains of the night on the floor, and this way I can sleep in reasonable comfort, and also make sure that you keep your promise too. You are too fond of running away, *chica*, and if I lie with my arm round you—so—I can make sure that you will still be here in the morning.'

He slept eventually, the unhurried regularity of his breathing told Nicola that, but she could not. She lay in the darkness, staring ahead of her, trying to come to terms with the fate that her rashness had apparently proved. Luis' arm was heavy across her, and she hated the promise of possession that it implied, but she was afraid to push it away lest she woke him.

When the first light came through the window, she turned her head slightly and watched him, wondering how she could ever have been such a fool as to mistake him for anyone else. But he was far removed from the plump middle-aged grandee of her imagination, or the ogre who haunted Teresita. Relaxed in sleep, a hint of stubble along his jaw, and long eyelashes curving on his cheek, he looked even younger than his years.

If Teresita had ever seen him like this, she thought wryly, then things might have been very different. As it was, she had only seen the power, the sexual charisma, and felt crushed by it.

Nicola could understand her fears only too well. She remembered the strength of the arms which had taken her prisoner so easily, and shivered. He had told her she could fight him by day, but he meant with words. Physically, he would always be the master, yet she could oppose him with her mind, and she would.

He might take, she thought fiercely, but she would never give. He would possess her body, but she would never surrender her spirit. She dared not, because the eventual desolation when his passion dwindled into indifference would be too much to bear.

Eventually she must have slept, because the next thing she remembered was Luis shaking her shoulder gently.

She sat up with a gasp as the events of the past night came flooding back.

'It is time we were on our way,' he said.

Her eyes were enormous as she looked at him. He had stripped to the waist, presumably to wash, and she wasn't proof against the potent masculine attraction of his lean golden-brown body. She made herself look away, wondering as she did so how many other women had lain in bed and watched him dress with the same hungry excitement leaping inside them.

She asked huskily, 'Is—is there any water?'

'I have warmed some for you, *querida*. I used cold. Have your wash while I saddle Malagueno.' He pulled on his shirt and began to fasten it as he walked to the door.

Nicola was thankful she didn't have to leave the shelter of the blanket in front of him. Her scraps of underwear were altogether too revealing, and the fact that he would soon have the right to see her without even that elementary covering made no difference at all.

She rinsed her face and hands swiftly, and dragged on her dress, jerking at the zip in her haste. The table was bare, and her shoulder bag, as she lifted it, empty except for cosmetics. Money, tickets, passport, everything had presumably passed into Luis' keeping. No possible avenue of retreat was being left open, she realised. She draped the folded blanket over her arm and went to the door. It was still early morning, and the sun hung low in the sky, a huge orange ball. The air was cool, and she breathed it gratefully.

Luis appeared leading Malagueno. '*Vamos, querida.* We can be at La Mariposa in time for breakfast.'

She gasped, 'So soon? But it must be miles away!'

'It is closer than you think,' he said drily. 'Your tracks were easier to follow than your route, which seemed to go in circles. Have you got all your things?'

'Those that have been left to me, yes,' she said coldly, then remembered. 'Oh—the driver's jacket. I can't leave that.'

When she reappeared, Luis took it from her.

'I was going to wear it,' Nicola protested.

His mouth hardened. 'You do not wear a garment belonging to another man. If you feel cold, take this.' He handed her the poncho he had been wearing the night before, and reluctantly she slipped it on.

As he lifted her into the saddle in front of him as he had done the previous night, she wondered if he would kiss her, hold her closely as they rode together. But he did not. In fact they might have been strangers.

But that's what we are, she thought, shivering in spite of the enveloping folds of the poncho. I'm going to marry a man I hardly know—someone I've only spent a few hours with.

It was a frightening thought, but on its heels came the even more disturbing realisation that if she had the chance to escape again, she was not sure that she would take it. And the implications of that kept her thoughtful all the way to the *hacienda*.

There was inevitably a reception committee waiting in the entrance hall of the *hacienda*. Nicola was deeply conscious of Luis' hand under her arm, urging her forward. On the fringe were several servants, all trying to be unobtrusive, but clearly eager to catch a glimpse of the girl who was to marry the *dueno*.

She drew a deep and shaky breath as she assimilated precisely who was waiting to receive her. She could hear Luis performing introductions, his tone cool and composed as if this was a perfectly conventional meeting.

'May I present my aunt, Doña Isabella de Costanza, my cousin Pilar, and her brother Ramón.'

She was aware of hostility in two pairs of dark feminine eyes, knew that the murmured welcome was words alone. But Ramón was altogether different. He stepped forward beaming.

'*Señorita*, may I welcome you to this house which is your home.'

His English was hesitant and deeply accented. Luis shot him a caustic look.

'Don't struggle, *amigo*. She speaks our language fluently.'

Doña Isabella stepped forward. Her bearing was regal, and her face stony as she looked at Nicola.

'No doubt you will wish to go to your room, *señorita*. I have assigned Maria to wait on you. When you are ready she will bring you to the *comedor* for breakfast.'

As she walked towards the stairs, following the pretty girl who had shyly come forward at Doña Isabella's imperious nod, Nicola tried to take in something of her surroundings.

The *hacienda* itself, she had thought as they approached, was more like a fortress, a rambling low building protected by a high wall. The family living quarters, it seemed were built in a large square round an interior courtyard, with separate wings for guests, and for the staff. Inside, the *hacienda* was incredibly spacious and cool, the fierceness of the sun being kept at bay by shutters on the windows. The floors were tiled, and such furniture as Nicola had glimpsed was clearly very old, opulently carved in dark wood.

She followed Maria along a wide corridor to a pair of double doors at the end. The girl pushed them open and stood back to allow Nicola to precede her into the room.

Nicola paused to look around her, her lips parting in sheer delight. It was a large room, and its charm lay in its utter simplicity, she thought. The walls were washed in a pale cream shade, and the highly polished furniture had probably made the journey to the New World from Spain in the sixteenth century. The bed was enormous, with four carved posts, and a cream silk counterpane embroidered lavishly with butterflies in green, pink, gold and silver. Hanging at the back of the bed was a huge embroidered panel in the shape of a butterfly, using the same colours as the bedcover.

Nicola thought, 'La Mariposa—of course!'

Maria smoothed the counterpane with an almost proprietorial air.

'This was the room of Doña Micaela, the mother of Don Luis, *señorita*,' she volunteered in a hushed tone. 'And before her, may God grant her peace, it was the room of his grandmother. Always the mistress of the *hacienda* has slept in this room.'

And the master? Nicola wanted to ask. Where does he sleep? She looked across at the wide bed, imagining generations of Spanish-born brides lying there, waiting and wondering if the door would open to admit their husbands.

And soon she too would lie waiting in the shadow of the butterfly.

'The bathroom, *señorita*,' Maria announced proudly, and Nicola turned away, thankful to have another focus for her attention. It was a charming bathroom, probably converted originally from a dressing room, tiled in jade and ivory, and including a shower cabinet among its luxurious appointments. Nicola noticed toiletries ranged on the shelves, all brand new, the seals on the flasks and jars unbroken, most of them made by names which a girl earning her own living had only heard of. It was a room dedicated to beauty, and to the art of making oneself beautiful for the appreciation of a man, and it made Nicola feel slightly sick. A little cage, she thought, where the bird can sit and preen herself all day.

But the thought of the shower was an irresistible temptation. Her hair was like straw, and she needed a change of clothes. She groaned inwardly as she remembered that the only luggage available to her was Teresita's. The Mexican girl had hastily filled a couple of cases from her vast wardrobe, in spite of Nicola's protests.

'You must have luggage with you, Nicky, or it will seem suspicious,' she had said. 'And all these are things I no longer need, so that you may leave them behind you when you run away.'

All the clothes now hanging in the cupboards and filling the drawers were elegant and expensive, but few of the styles or the colours were what she would have chosen for herself, and the thought of having to present herself downstairs in another girl's dress to the scornful looks of Doña Isabella and Pilar was unpleasant.

The next shock was that Maria clearly considered it

her duty to assist Nicola with her shower. Nicola spent several minutes firmly disabusing the girl of this notion, and dismissed her, promising that she would ring if she needed anything.

The shower was delicious and she revelled in it, letting the warm water stream through her hair and down her body. She wrapped herself in a fluffy bath sheet, tucking it round her body like a sarong as she came back into the room. No doubt somewhere there would be some means of drying her hair, but she was reluctant to ring for Maria again. She needed to be on her own for a while.

She sat down on the stool in front of the dressing chest and stared at herself. Could this really be happening? It seemed impossible. Tomorrow or the next day she should have been in Merida, preparing to start her holiday, and instead she was here in this beautiful room, a virtual prisoner.

And somewhere in this house was the man who had made her his prisoner. The man she had promised to marry. She swallowed, fighting back the bubble of hysteria rising in her throat. It was all a monstrous joke—it had to be. She was no demure Spanish dove accepting the gilded cage provided for her, and offering in return her duty and obedience to a comparative stranger.

Not love, she thought, but compliance, surrendering herself to her master's will, but making no demands of her own. Asking no questions.

Men like Luis de Montalba—men like Ewan— expected the wives they had married for convenience to look discreetly the other way while they amused themselves. She wondered whether Greta had learned her lesson yet, and whether it had been a painful one for her. Yet perhaps she simply regarded it as part of the price she had paid for Ewan. Because she wanted him, and always had.

Nicola had seen the hungry way in which the rather blank blue eyes had fastened on him from the first. She had even laughed about it with Ewan, secure in the knowledge that it was herself he wanted to be alone with, to hold in his arms. The possibility that that was all he might want had never entered her head, although it should have done, because she had recognised from the first that he was ambitious, and had even applauded it.

Well, at least Teresita was going to be spared that kind of misery, Nicola thought. She had Cliff, and they loved each other, and although nothing was certain in this uncertain world, they had the chance to be happy together. Teresita wouldn't have to spend her life dutifully bearing children and being moved from one expensive prison to another.

She shivered convulsively, pressing her clenched fist against her mouth.

Was this the fate she had brought upon herself when she had unthinkingly embarked on her masquerade?

She reached for her hairbrush and pushing back the stool went towards the window. She unfastened the shutter and stepped out on to a balcony running, she saw, the whole length of the first floor. The heat of the sun was like a blow, and she closed her eyes against its fierceness, moving her shoulders in sensuous pleasure as she pulled the brush through her hair, lifting the soft strands to dry them.

She heard a sound below her and looking down saw that Ramón was standing in the courtyard beneath, his expression a mixture of admiration and embarrassment.

'I did not mean to disturb you,' he said. 'I was on my way to the stables.' He gestured towards a gated archway in the corner of the courtyard.

'You're not disturbing me at all,' she said lightly. 'I've been washing my hair.'

'As I can see. It's very beautiful.' He smiled at her, and Nicola found herself warming to him. He had an attraction all his own, she thought. He was shorter than Luis, and swarthier, and his features were less aquiline, but he possessed an open friendly charm, and Nicola knew that a journey of several days in a car with him would have been pleasant without posing any problems at all.

As if reading her thoughts, he said ruefully 'Luis has the luck of the devil himself.'

She felt herself flushing. 'Then you know—everything?'

He spread his hands, shrugging. 'Luis telephoned me from the first stop he made. He wished me to check on Teresita on his behalf. He could hardly do so without telling me what had happened, although . . .' He stopped suddenly.

'Although you never expected that he would bring me here,' Nicola supplied drily.

It was his turn to flush. 'Well—perhaps not. But I am delighted, I assure you. It is time he was married. He has been lonely, I think.'

Nicola lifted her eyebrows. 'That's not the word I would have chosen.'

'Señorita Tarrant!' He looked more flustered than ever. 'He is only a man after all, not a saint. And besides . . .'

'Besides, I shouldn't know such things,' she finished for him, making herself smile. 'And please call me Nicola.'

He smiled too, delighted and plainly relieved at the shift in the conversation. 'I shall be pleased to do so. I hope we can be friends.'

'I hope so too.' She looked around. 'This courtyard is charming.'

There was a well in the centre, with a stone seat around it, and above it a parched-looking tree providing shade. Nicola wondered whether the well held water, but looking at the brazen sky she was inclined to think it was purely decorative.

'I am glad you like it,' said Ramón. 'It is cool here in the evenings, which makes it a pleasant place to sit. And when there are parties, the servants hang lanterns in the tree, and around the gallery.'

'Are there many such parties?'

'Not for some time, but all that will change now.'

He meant there would be celebrations in honour of Don Luis' marriage, she thought. Well, as far as she was concerned, the lanterns would remain in storage for the foreseeable future. Yet, she could imagine how the courtyard would look when it was lit by the lights from the house, and the tree, instead of the glare of the sun, and when perhaps a golden moon swung above it in the night sky. There would be exotic foods laid out on white-clothed tables, and the enticing smell of meat grilling over charcoal. And above the murmur of voices and laughter, the swish of silks and the flutter of fans, would rise the sound of a *mariachi* band.

It was all so real that for a moment Nicola felt dazed, as if she had suffered a time-slip—as if the *hacienda* was speaking to her in some strange way.

What nonsense, she told herself forcibly. She was merely suffering from the combined effects of emotional stress, a bad night, and an empty stomach.

She watched Ramón cross the courtyard and disappear under the arch, then turned back into her room, running her fingers through her hair to test its dampness as she did so.

She came face to face with Luis who was standing, hands on hips, waiting for her, his face set in grim lines.

He said coldly, 'My aunt is waiting to order breakfast to be served. I came to see what had detained you.'

She said, 'I'm sorry, I washed my hair. I went outside to dry it.'

'And to talk to my cousin Ramón.' He paused. 'Perhaps in future you would wait to converse with him until you are fully dressed.'

Nicola glanced down at herself, then looked at him incredulously. She was fully covered from the top of her breasts down to her feet.

She said heatedly, 'I'm perfectly decent. I'm wearing a damned sight more now than I was last night!'

His voice became icier than ever. 'What you wear, or do not wear, for my eyes only is a different matter. You will please remember that. Now Tia Isabella is waiting.' He turned on his heel and left the room, leaving Nicola staring after him, torn between anger and amusement.

Anger won. 'Who the hell does he think he is?' she raged inwardly, snatching a handful of filmy underwear from a drawer and dragging a dress from a hanger.

But the answer was already formulating in her mind. He was her captor, her jailer, the man with the key to her prison, the man who made his wishes known and was quite capable of enforcing them.

She swallowed, and her hands clenched, her nails digging into the soft flesh of her palms.

She thought, 'Dear God, I've got to escape from here before it's too late.'

CHAPTER FIVE

NICOLA's face was set and mutinous as she sat in the shade of the gallery. A chair and a footstool had been set for her there by Carlos, the grizzled-haired martinet who appeared to be the household's major-domo, and a table bearing a tray with a jug of iced fresh fruit juice and a glass was to hand, but she ignored it.

Breakfast had been a horrendous meal from beginning to end. Entering the *comedor* in Carlos' wake had been like walking headlong into a brick wall of hostility.

Luis' eyes had looked her over coolly and swiftly, assimilating the ill-fitting bodice and loose skirt of the dress she was wearing, and she saw his mouth tighten in exasperation.

He said, 'Tia Isabella, Nicola needs a new wardrobe. Perhaps you would arrange for your dressmaker to be sent for.'

'I have plenty of clothes of my own,' Nicola protested. 'They're just—elsewhere.'

He shrugged. 'And there they can remain. In any event they would hardly make a suitable trousseau.'

Nicola sank down into the chair he was holding for her, hearing Doña Isabella draw in a swift breath like the hiss of a snake.

She said, 'Luis, you cannot expect . . .'

'But I do expect,' he said softly. 'I thought I had made that clear.'

There was a silence like knives, and Nicola stared down at the polished surface of the table. She glanced up and encountered an inimical glance from Pilar which brought the colour into her cheeks. She was a pretty girl, but the sullen expression, which seemed habitual, spoiled her looks.

'My nephew informs me that his marriage to you will take place as soon as the arrangements can be made,' Doña Isabella broke the silence at last, her gaze resting pointedly on Nicola's waistline. 'It will naturally be a very quiet wedding.'

'On the contrary,' Luis said coolly. 'Invitations will be sent to the entire family, and to our friends.'

Doña Isabella gasped, her back becoming, if possible, more rigid than ever. 'But under the circumstances—the very doubtful circumstances ...' She floundered to a halt with a suddenly martyred air. 'As you wish, Luis, of course.'

'Thank you, Tia Isabella,' he bowed. He glanced at Nicola. 'Your own family, *querida*. Can they be persuaded to make the journey, do you think?'

She moved her shoulders helplessly. 'My father is a farmer. This is a busy time for him—and my mother certainly wouldn't come without him. I just don't know.'

'But when you write to them, you will offer the invitation.' It wasn't a question, it was a command, she knew. Her mind closed completely when she tried to imagine how she was going to break the news to her family—what she could say.

'So you are a farmer's daughter?' Pilar spoke for the first time, her tone openly insolent. 'How sad that Luis spends so little time at the *hacienda*. You would feel quite at home among the cattle and horses.'

Nicola smiled lightly. 'And pigs,' she said. 'I feel quite at home with them too.'

There was a startled hush as Pilar digested this, then an angry flush mounted in her face and she gave Nicola a venomous look. Another sharp silence descended, and a look stolen under her lashes told Nicola that Luis' face was icy with displeasure at the interchange.

Carlos came into the room followed by a uniformed maid. Coffee was placed on the table, and warm rolls, and then an enormous dish of scrambled eggs mixed with finely minced onion, tomato and chili appeared. Nicola was hungry, but she had to force each forkful down her throat. As she ate, she allowed herself gradually to look round the room, and take in her surroundings. It had a somewhat repressive atmosphere, the dark heavy furniture giving a feeling of solidity and stability, as if reminding the onlooker that this house, this land had been wrested from the wilderness centuries before, and that the Montalbas had set their hand and seal over it. This impression was deepened by the family portraits which hung in gloomy splendour round the walls.

It was inbred in them all, and had been from the beginning, she thought, that look of cool arrogance. Dark patrician faces looked down in command from every canvas, proclaiming their lordship of this New World they had made their own. And the women were cast in the same mould, she thought ruefully. They sat staring rigidly into space, their hands disposed to show their beautiful rings, their rich lace mantillas decorously draped over high combs, expressionless, guarded and without visible emotion.

All except one, and Nicola found her gaze returning to this particular portrait over and over again, fascinated by the wilful expression in the dark eyes, and the faint smile playing about the full lips which seemed to deny the studied decorum of the pose. She was obviously much younger than most of the other women depicted, and while none of them looked as if they had ever given their respective husbands even a moment's anxiety, this girl seemed as if she might have been quite a handful for any strait-laced grandee.

Instead of the conventional head-covering, she wore a silver butterfly gleaming against her dark tresses, and in one hand she held a dark red rose which provided a dramatic contrast against the silvery brocade of her gown.

Nicola would have liked to have asked about her, but it was unlikely that Doña Isabella or Pilar would wish to enlighten her, and Luis was frowningly examining a pile of mail which Carlos had just presented to him and was clearly preoccupied.

When the meal was over, he excused himself abruptly and left the room, and after a moment Doña Isabella rose too, followed by Pilar, leaving Nicola sitting alone at the big rectangular table.

She bit her lip as the door closed behind them, but reminded herself that she could have expected little else. She was unwelcome here, an interloper, and if it was any consolation Teresita would probably have fared little better.

Eventually Carlos had found her loitering rather uncertainly in the hall, and had installed her with a certain amount of ceremony on the shaded terrace which encircled the courtyard.

But I can't sit here for ever, she thought. There must be something I can do.

She looked across to the archway. The stables were through there somewhere, and she supposed there would be no real objection to her visiting them, exploring a little on her own account. She rose, and moved slowly and languidly along the terrace to the archway. It was as she had thought. She could see other buildings, rather less impressive than the *hacienda* itself, and in the distance she could hear a vague hum of voices, and an occasional shrill laugh. She thought she could also hear the faint strum of a guitar, but perhaps that was her imagination.

She pushed open the gate and walked through, half expecting to be intercepted and sent back where she belonged, but if anyone had observed her arrival they gave no sign, and she wandered on without interference.

The kitchens seemed to be a separate wing altogether, she thought, her nose wrinkling appreciatively at the appetising aromas drifting towards her. Everyone would be far too busy preparing the massive midday meal to worry about her.

She crossed another courtyard and turned a corner, her eyes widening as she came upon what seemed to be a small village street lined with single-storey cabins. Washing dried in the sun, and a group of small children played in the dust—some complicated and absorbing game with flat stones she noted as she passed.

She smiled, and said, '*Buenos dias*,' but they gaped at her in silence, clearly disconcerted by her appearance among them.

Nicola walked on slowly. Two separate communities, she thought, occupying the same limited space, and totally interdependent. Don Luis appeared to look after his workers well, she admitted grudgingly. The cabins were well built and properly maintained and there was a feeling of tranquillity pervading the entire street.

When she reached the end, she paused, uncertain which way to take next. A dog, lying in the shadow of a wall, lifted its head and barked with the air of an animal prepared to go through the motions, and no more.

Nicola grinned to herself. 'Love and peace, man,' she said half under her breath. She paused and looked around her, shading her eyes with her hand. Over to the right, she could see cultivated land, streaked with irrigation channels, and men working there, so she turned left instead, and found herself in yet another courtyard surrounded by stable buildings. Ramón was there, talking to a small squat man in a broad-brimmed hat. He broke off as he caught sight of her and came across immediately.

'Señorita—Nicola. What are you doing here? Is Luis not with you?'

'I decided to take a look round,' she said, evading the question. 'Isn't it permitted.'

He smiled. 'Of course—this is your home. Perhaps if we can persuade you to like it, then Luis would spend more time here.'

She said drily, 'Please don't overestimate my influence with your cousin.'

Ramón laughed. 'How could I?' He paused, sobering a little. 'Perhaps I should explain. Luis loves La Mariposa and always has done, but in recent years he has spent less and less time here—and not altogether because of his business commitments.' He hesitated. 'It is difficult for me to say this, but Madrecita—my mother and Luis have not always—agreed as I would wish. He is good to her, of course. For years she has been the mistress here, but now that he is to marry all that will change.' He grimaced slightly. 'If—if there was anything—lacking in her welcome, perhaps you can understand. And also she had certain plans of her own . . .'

'She wanted Luis to marry Pilar,' Nicola translated, and he looked embarrassed.

'She did. It was nonsense, of course. Luis had never given any indication—and Pilar herself would never have thought—except . . .'

He paused again, and Nicola prompted, 'Except?'

Ramón sighed. 'Why should you not know? My sister is young and impressionable. A year ago she formed—an attachment for a man, but it was unsuitable, and she was told to think no more of him. At the same time, my mother began to suggest . . .' He shrugged. 'I am sure I need say no more.'

Nicola said ruefully, 'I see.' Poor Pilar, she thought. A double loser. No wonder she had sensed that white-hot resentment!

'Do you think she was—in love with Luis?' she asked.

'I doubt it,' he said. 'He never gave her the least encouragement. I think she was—prepared to be in love with love, for the sake of being mistress of—all this.' He spread his arms wide. 'Not that this is all of it, by any means, as you must know.'

'I know very little,' Nicola confessed. 'Only what Teresita told me.'

'Ah yes. From what Luis told me, I understand you shared an apartment with her.' He smiled reminiscently. 'A sweet child.'

'She spoke well of you too.'

'She did?' He seemed pleased. 'And yet she can have little reason to remember this place or any of us with much pleasure. Her visit was a disaster. She was frightened of horses, and Luis, thinking to please her, took her up on his saddle. *Ay de mi*!' He gave a groan. 'First she cried and screamed, then she was sick.'

'How clever of her,' Nicola said acidly. 'I wish I'd tried the same thing myself.'

Ramón gave her a puzzled look. 'You too are afraid of horses? That is sad—Luis is an expert horseman.'

'I've ridden since childhood.'

He beamed at her. 'Then that will please him greatly.'

Nicola bit her lip. 'Pleasing your cousin is not the sole object of my life.'

His smile vanished altogether. 'But as his wife . . .'

'We're not married yet,' Nicola said tautly.

'But you will be. Luis is a man of his word.'

'And that's all that matters? Don't my wishes come into this?'

'I had assumed that in this your wishes would coincide with his.' Ramón looked embarrassed. 'You must consider, Nicola, the circumstances of your meeting—all that has happened since.' He paused. 'When Luis telephoned me to say that you had taken Teresita's place, it was clear he had—certain intentions towards you.'

She felt slow colour rising in her face. She strove to make her voice casual. 'But not marriage?'

'No—not then. But something clearly has happened to change his mind and . . .'

'Nothing has happened,' she interrupted. 'For heaven's sake, it isn't a question of honour—his, mine or anyone else's. You must believe me.'

'It is not my affair,' he said flatly. 'I should not have spoken at all. Forgive me. You came to see the horses. Will you permit me to show them to you? There is, alas, only one suitable for a woman to ride and that belongs to my sister Pilar.' He added without any real conviction, 'I am sure she would be happy to lend her to you if you wished.'

Nicola took pity on him. 'If I want to go riding, then I'll ask her. What I'd really like is to have a look around the *hacienda*. It's so old that I'm sure it must have a fascinating history.'

'Oh, it has.' Ramón cheered up perceptibly. 'I would be happy to escort you—perhaps later, after luncheon?'

She smiled and nodded before turning away. For a moment it had occurred to her that it might be possible to enlist Ramón's support in getting away from here, but she had already thought better of that idea. Ramón was his cousin's man to the last degree. It had been apparent in every word, every inflection in his voice. There was no help for her there—or anywhere else, for that matter.

Ramón obviously thought she was a very fortunate lady, she told herself wryly as she made her way slowly back to the house. He thought Luis had seduced her either on the way here or the previous night, and was making honourable amends. She remembered Doña Isabella's gimlet stare and grimaced.

Maria was hovering on the terrace when she returned. 'The Señor Don Luis has instructed me to make alterations in some of your dresses, *señorita*. If you would come upstairs and show me those you wish me to begin on.'

The girl sounded a little subdued, and Nicola wondered with a pang whether she had been told off for not taking better care of her new mistress. She could hardly explain that she just wasn't used to having a maid. But it was a fact that she could use Maria's services. She was no hand with a needle, and never had been, and it was no fun walking round in clothes which patently didn't fit her even as a gesture of defiance.

Going through Teresita's dresses and choosing those that could be adapted to her needs filled in the time before lunch quite adequately. Maria bloomed with new importance. She sighed with admiration over the colour of Nicola's hair, but shook her head at its condition. She also hinted that Nicola was too thin. Perhaps the Señor Don Luis' taste ran to plumper women, Nicola deduced with exasperation from the girl's demure smile.

She told herself that it was a matter of indifference to her what his tastes in that direction might be, but believing it was a different matter. Unwillingly she remembered that first evening at the motel—the way those women tourists had watched him—the odd pang she had felt . . .

Resolutely, Nicola closed her mind against that. All she needed to recall now was that he was the man who was forcing her into an unwanted loveless marriage to satisfy his injured pride. Not that that was the sole satisfaction he required, she thought, suddenly dry-mouthed as she remembered the searing effect of his lips and hands, the little shaken storm of desire he had so effortlessly aroused in her.

And Maria had her orders, she thought, to make sure that the bride was desirable at all times because the *dueno*'s will was paramount.

She had no wish at all to go down to lunch, but nor did she wish to face the inevitable questions, probably from Don Luis himself, if she remained in her room. Her blue dress had been returned, freshly laundered and pressed, and she changed into it with a feeling of relief.

When she entered the *comedor*, an instant silence fell, forcing her to the conclusion that she had been the subject under discussion, and she checked for a moment, flushing a little, until Ramón's friendly smile welcomed her.

Luis wasn't there, she discovered, looking round her.

'My cousin apologises for his tardiness,' Ramón told her in an undertone. 'He is interviewing one Pablo who drives a truck.' He gave her a conspiratorial side-glance.

'A truck driver?' Pilar's ears were as sharp as her voice

Say Hello to Yesterday

Holly Weston had done it all alone.

She had raised her small son and worked her way up to features writer for a major newspaper. Still the bitterness of the the past seven years lingered.

She had been very young when she married Nick Falconer—but old enough to lose her heart completely when he left. Despite her success in her new life, her old one haunted her.

But it was over and done with—until an assignment in Greece brought her face to face with Nick, and all she was trying to forget. . . .

Time of the Temptress

The game must be played his way!

Rebellion against a cushioned, controlled life had landed Eve Tarrant in Africa. Now only the tough mercenary Wade O'Mara stood between her and possible death in the wild, revolution-torn jungle.

But the real danger was Wade himself—he had made Eve aware of herself as a woman.

"I saved your neck, so you feel you owe me something," Wade said. "But you don't owe me a thing, Eve. Get away from me." She knew she could make him lose his head if she tried. But that wouldn't solve anything. . . .

Your Romantic Adventure Starts Here.

Born Out of Love

It had to be coincidence!

Charlotte stared at the man through a mist of confusion. It was Logan. An older Logan, of course, but unmistakably the man who had ravaged her emotions and then abandoned her all those years ago.

She ought to feel angry. She ought to feel resentful and cheated. Instead, she was apprehensive—terrified at the complications he could create.

"We are not through, Charlotte," he told her flatly. "I sometimes think we haven't even begun."

Man's World

Kate was finished with love for good.

Kate's new boss, features editor Eliot Holman, might have devastating charms—but Kate couldn't care less, even if it was obvious that he was interested in her.

Everyone, including Eliot, thought Kate was grieving over the loss of her husband, Toby. She kept it a carefully guarded secret just how cruelly Toby had treated her and how terrified she was of trusting men again.

But Eliot refused to leave her alone, which only served to infuriate her. He was no different from any other man. . . or was he?

These FOUR free Harlequin Presents novels allow you to enter the world of romance, love and desire. As a member of the Harlequin Home Subscription Plan, you can continue to experience all the moods of love. You'll be inspired by moments so real...so moving...you won't want them to end. So start your own Harlequin Presents adventure by returning the reply card below. <u>DO IT TODAY!</u>

apparently. 'Why doesn't Juan Hernandez speak to such people?'

Ramón shrugged, clearly wishing he had said nothing. 'Because this is a matter which Luis prefers to deal with himself.'

Pilar subsided, but there was a speculative look in her eyes.

Thoroughly embarrassed, Nicola looked round her, and saw the portrait which had so intrigued her earlier. Surely it wasn't just a trick of the light that put such an expression of dancing mischief in the dark eyes as she surveyed her descendants.

'You are admiring Doña Manuela, little cousin?' Ramón leaned forward.

'Ramón!' his mother snapped. 'Please remember that there is as yet no established relationship between our family and—Señorita Tarrant.'

Ramón jerked a shoulder unabashed. 'The relationship will be established soon enough,' he said with an ill-concealed grin. 'If I were in Luis' shoes I would wait no longer than it takes for Father Gonzago to get here from the mission.'

'Well, you are not in his shoes, and never will be,' Doña Isabella's voice was even snappier. 'I must apologise for my son, señorita. His manners have apparently deserted him.'

'On the contrary,' Nicola said sweetly, 'Don Ramón has been all that is kind ever since I arrived here.'

Doña Isabella's frankly fulminating glance indicated that Don Ramón was an idiot, but she said nothing.

The door swung open and Luis strode in. 'My regrets for having kept you waiting. You should have told Carlos to begin serving.'

'It was of no importance,' Doña Isabella assured him with an acid smile.

'Why have you been talking to a truck driver?' Pilar demanded.

Luis lifted a shoulder in a cool shrug. 'I found myself

in his debt, and preferred to repay him in person. I am grateful to you, Pilar, for this concern in my affairs,' he added silkily. 'But perhaps we can now consider the matter closed.'

Pilar's eyes flashed mutinously, but she said nothing as the door opened to admit Carlos bearing a large silver tureen of soup.

It was a delicious meal from the soup itself, full of spicy meatballs and aromatic with herbs, to the pork cooked with chili and vegetables and served on a heaped bed of rice, and ending with *cocada*—a concoction of syrupy, sherry-flavoured coconut.

Many more meals like that, and all Maria's wishes about her figure would be fulfilled, Nicola thought wryly as she put down her napkin.

'You like Mexican cooking, Señorita Tarrant?' Pilar leaned forward, smiling with patent insincerity. 'I thought our food would have been too warm, too highly spiced for pallid Anglo-Saxon tastes.'

If food were all that she was talking about, Nicola thought with sudden anger. She said, 'But you forget that I've been in Mexico for more than a year. I've had plenty of time to accustom myself.' She turned to Ramón, smiling at him. 'Please don't forget you promised to show me the *hacienda*.'

'Certainly.' Ramón rose gallantly. He looked at Luis, leaning back in his chair at the head of the table, his dark face enigmatic. 'You permit, Luis?'

'You are the expert on the house, *amigo*.' His tone sounded bored, but Nicola sensed that he was not pleased, and found it oddly exciting.

As they crossed the hall, Ramón said with a trace of awkwardness, 'You may think it strange that my mother did not offer to act as your guide, but . . .'

'I don't find it strange at all,' she returned drily. 'I'm sure that she and your sister would much prefer to continue their listing of all the ways in which I fall short of being a suitable bride for your cousin.'

He sighed. 'So they make it so obvious? Nicola, I am truly sorry. In truth, my mother has become so accustomed to being the mistress here that she will find it hard to take second place to another woman—to any woman. It is not a personal thing, believe me.'

Nicola wasn't so sure, but she smiled at him. 'Thank you for the reassurance.' They were in the *salón*, and she glanced around, wanting to turn the conversation from the personal to the general for Ramón's sake as much as anything. He couldn't be blamed for his mother and sister's behaviour.

'What a beautiful room this is.' She made her words deliberately conventional. 'The furniture is very old, I suppose.'

'Most of it was brought from Spain on sailing ships and then hauled here on wagons drawn by mules.' He grimaced comically. 'What a journey! What an undertaking! It makes one feel ill to contemplate it even in these modern times.' He smiled. 'Doña Manuela must have had a singularly persuasive way with her.'

Nicola remembered that he had referred to the portrait she had admired earlier as Doña Manuela.

'Then it was all her doing?' She gestured round her.

'To a great extent,' Ramón nodded in confirmation. 'It is a romantic story. I am surprised that Luis himself did not wish to tell it to you. She was a great beauty and an heiress, but she fell in love with a soldier who had little but his own courage, so her family forbade her to think of him. She could have married anyone, it was said. She was used to court life, crowded gatherings, balls and festivals. She was a wonderful dancer, so light on her feet that she was called La Mariposa, the Butterfly.'

'Then the *hacienda* was named after her?'

'*Si*. Her lover became a *conquistador* and made himself a fortune. This time when he sought her hand, her family did not refuse, although they begged her not to come to this wild and primitive land—not to leave

Spain. And she laughed, and said that she would take a little of Spain with her.'

'She certainly did that.' Nicola's fingers moved appreciatively over the ancient, heavily carved wood. She wondered if the *hacienda* had altered very much from those days. It had developed, and become more luxurious with succeeding generations, but if Doña Manuela were here at this moment, walking beside them with her silk skirts rustling, it would probably still be familiar to her.

What could she have thought, coming from her pampered and cossetted background in Spain to this wilderness! Compared to a castle in Spain, the *hacienda* would have seemed primitive indeed to the *conquistador*'s bride. Had she still smiled as she rode in her wagon with her servants and outriders to protect her from the hostile Indians, or had even her lively spirit quailed as she contemplated what lay in front of her?

She asked, 'Was she happy here—after all that?'

Ramón shrugged. 'She did not have long to enjoy her happiness. She died in childbirth about a year after the portrait of her was completed, and her husband nearly went mad with grief. It was only the son she had borne him that saved his sanity.'

Nicola shivered. 'You said it was a romantic story. I think it's a sad one.'

He looked faintly surprised. 'Cannot it be both? To love and be beloved in return—isn't that what every woman secretly desires, no matter how short such happiness may be?'

Nicola said shortly, 'I wouldn't know. Shall we go on with the tour?'

There were numerous rooms on the ground floor, all graciously sized and quite sufficient to give any of the *hacienda*'s inhabitants as much privacy as any of them might desire. In fact Nicola couldn't imagine what half of them were used for, but Ramón seemed to take the opulence of his surroundings totally for granted.

The room she liked least was Luis's study. No concessions to luxury had been made there. It was a starkly masculine room, equipped with a workmanlike desk, and lined with books.

'This is Luis's sanctuary when he is here,' Ramón commented. 'It is a rule that no one interrupts him when that door is shut, but of course it will not apply to you, little cousin.'

'I can't imagine any exception being made in my case,' she said. The severe simplicity of it surprised her. She had expected something rather more hedonistic for the master. 'You don't share it with him?'

'*Dios*, no,' Ramón laughed. 'I have my own office. I don't intrude on Luis' privacy. I am not so brave.' He glanced at her quickly. 'But I think his solitude will not be so precious to him now.'

Solitude? Nicola questioned inwardly. Luis Alvarado de Montalba was the last person in the world who needed to be alone.

She turned to leave the room, and started violently as she saw him leaning in the doorway watching them. Ramón looked taken aback too.

'I'm sorry, Luis.' He spread his hands swiftly. 'But I thought you would wish Nicola to see everything—even here.'

'Of course.' He did not move. 'But it might be more appropriate if Carmela were to show her the kitchen quarters—and the bedrooms. Juan Hernandez is looking for you.'

'I'll go at once,' said Ramón. He disappeared before Nicola was even able to thank him.

Luis strolled past her to the desk and took a thin black cigar from a box there. He lit it unhurriedly, still watching her.

'Do you like my house, *querida*?'

She noticed he did not say 'home'.

'No one could help liking it,' she said, a little helplessly. She paused. 'Ramón told me about Doña

Manuela—La Mariposa. I wondered about her, when I saw the butterfly in her hair.'

'It is said he had it made for her,' he said. 'From silver mined near Santo Tomás.'

'Does it still exist?'

He shook his head. 'I believe it was buried with her.' His hand moved towards one of the telephones on the desk—the house phone, she guessed. 'Shall I summon Carmela to show you the rest of the place?'

'Not—not for a moment.' She swallowed. 'I must talk to you.'

Luis blew a reflective cloud of smoke. 'I am at your service, *amiga.*'

Nicola took a deep breath. 'It's hopeless—you must see that. Keeping me here—marrying me—just won't work. Your family will never accept me as your wife. It would be better—much easier for everyone if you—let me go.'

'Easier for you perhaps,' he said drily. 'But I have no intention of letting you go. However, you need not fear. Tia Isabella will mellow to you in time. She has too much to lose if she does not,' he added cynically.

She stared at him. 'I don't understand.'

'It is simple enough. Her husband had money, but he was a gambler, a speculator in minerals. He invested heavily in mines which yielded nothing, and lost everything. Fortunately the shock killed him before Tia Isabella had a chance to do so. As Ramón's passion had always been ranching, and not ill-starred investments, it seemed sensible to offer him La Mariposa as his home and allow him to run it for me. But Tia Isabella is my guest here, and only my guest, as I was forced to remind her.'

She moistened her lips. 'You told Ramón the truth—about how we met, and other things—but what did you tell your aunt and your cousin?'

His mouth twisted. 'Not the truth, *chica,* but a story to fit the circumstances. Does it matter?'

'I suppose not,' she said defeatedly.

He took her chin in his hand, forcing her to look up at him. 'A word of warning. Do not make my cousin Ramón fall in love with you. I should not find it amusing.'

'I don't find any of this particularly amusing,' she snapped, pulling away from him. 'But you don't have to worry. With an unwanted bridegroom in my life, I'm not likely to start encouraging anyone else!'

She turned to leave, but he gripped her arm, pulling her round to face him.

'So you don't want me,' he said softly. 'What a little hypocrite you are, *amiga*.'

He bent his head and found her lips with his. This time there was no savagery, no coercion. His mouth moved slowly and persuasively on hers, coaxing her lips apart in a sensually teasing caress which sent her blood hammering through her veins. All her good resolutions about remaining aloof and unbending died a swift death as he drew her closer against the hardness of his body, his own urgency firing a response she was helpless to control.

She thought, 'I never knew it could be like this. God help me, I never knew . . .' Then all thinking processes were suspended as her awareness yielded totally to these new sensations he was evoking in her. Her hands linked behind his neck, her fingers curling into his thick dark hair, and eyes closed, she swayed against him, blind and deaf to everything but the clamour of her body as his kiss deepened endlessly.

Pilar said from the doorway, 'Luis, is your telephone switched off? There is a call for you . . . Oh!'

Without any great haste, he lifted his head and looked at her.

'*Gracias*, Pilar. Perhaps you would be good enough to find Carmela and tell her that my *novia* is anxious to be shown the rest of the house.'

Pilar gave a little sniff and turned on her heel to leave,

sending, as she did so, a look at Nicola which combined the usual hostility with a kind of shocked curiosity.

Nicola's face burned as she stepped back, her hands going up to smooth her dishevelled hair.

When she was sure Pilar was no longer within earshot, she said unsteadily, 'I hate you.'

He smiled. 'Perhaps, *querida*, but at least you are not indifferent to me.'

'I'll be working on it,' she whispered, staring at him.

He shrugged slightly, his amused gaze roaming over her flushed face, and the swift rise and fall of her breasts under the tight fitting bodice. 'What a waste of energy, *querida*, that might be employed in more—agreeable ways. And now, if you will excuse me . . .' He reached for the telephone.

Nicola longed to slam the door as she left the room, but it was too heavy and solid, resisting her efforts to close it even, so that she had ample time to hear his soft-voiced, '*Si*? Carlota, how is it with you?'

She stood in the corridor outside, staring at the heavy timbers which prevented her hearing any more, and knowing a childish desire to beat on them with her convulsively clenched fists.

The unknown caller had to be Carlota Garcia, the woman Teresita had mentioned. She had assumed the affair was in the past, but it seemed she was mistaken. Luis had not the slightest intention of allowing a little thing like marriage to interfere with his chosen pleasures. The sudden ache in her throat made her feel as if she was swallowing past knives, and yet what had she really expected?

She began to run down the corridor. In the hall, she encountered Carmela, a stout woman with greying hair whose ready smile faded to puzzlement and sympathy as Nicola explained that she had a headache and would not be seeing any more of the *hacienda* that day. She refused all offers of cool drinks and medication, and fled upstairs to her room.

But even there, there was no sanctuary. She lay on the wide bed and looked up at the butterfly, its delicate embroidered wings shimmering in the sunlight. Her emblem was everywhere—this girl who had travelled half across the world to find her love.

Nicola thought, 'I've travelled as far—but what is there here for me? No love, certainly.'

There were tears on her face, but she welcomed them, knowing that, without love, she would one day know a bitterness too deep for tears, and wondering, with a kind of despair, why she should suddenly be so sure of this.

By the time Maria arrived to help her to dress for dinner, she had regained some measure of control. Maria had brought with her the dress she had been altering, a simple black sheath, with a deep square neckline and elbow-length sleeves. Dressed in it, Nicola felt prepared to face the world, if not enjoy it. She had finished doing her face under Maria's approving scrutiny and was applying some gloss to her lips, when there was a knock at the door.

Maria went to answer it, and stood aside giggling as Luis walked in. Then, before Nicola could stop her, she vanished, leaving them alone together.

She sat staring into the mirror, watching him approach. He came and stood behind her.

He said, 'I regret, *querida*, that I shall not be here for dinner. I have to go to Santo Tomás quite unexpectedly.'

Nicola replaced the cap on the tube of glosser and put it down. She was pleased to see how steady her hands were.

'Have you nothing to say?' His eyes watched hers in the mirror.

'What do you want me to say?'

He shrugged. 'Just a word that you are sorry—that you might even miss me.'

She said without a trace of expression, 'I'm sorry. I shall miss you,' and saw his mouth tighten.

He said, 'I had intended to give you this later, but I thought perhaps you might wish to wear it at dinner—as a reminder of me,' he added cynically.

He put a flat velvet case on the dressing table in front of her. For a moment she didn't move, and he said with a trace of impatience, 'Open it, *amiga*.'

It was a pendant, a single lustrous pearl on a long golden chain. Nicola had never seen anything so lovely. As she stared at it, she felt as if she could scarcely breathe.

He leaned over her shoulder and lifted it out of its satin bed. He put the chain round her neck, and the pearl slid coolly into the hidden shadowed valley between her breasts. Luis bent and put his lips to the curve of her shoulder.

If she had been calm before, then she was trembling now, her pulses hammering at the slightest brush of his mouth on her body.

He said softly, 'It matches your skin, *querida*.' His hands moved on her shoulders, sliding the dress away from her.

Nicola said, 'No,' hoarsely, and her hands came up, snatching at the material to cover her breasts.

He frowned a little. 'Don't be frightened, *amada*. I only want to look at you—not touch—or kiss. I shall keep my word. But when you are my wife, and perhaps less shy of me, then you can wear it as I wish—with nothing to hide either the pearl—or you—from me.'

Slowly, almost mockingly he readjusted her dress. He said, 'Aren't you going to thank me?'

Nicola said coolly, '*Gracias, señor*. It's very lovely. I'm sure Teresita would have been delighted with it too.'

The dark face hardened, and he straightened abruptly. She expected some stinging retort, and closed her eyes as if to shield herself from his anger. But none came, and when she ventured to look, he was alone.

Her legs were shaking as she got up from the stool at

last. She got downstairs somehow, and into the *salón* where they were waiting for her.

She said, 'I'm sorry if I'm late.'

Ramón came forward drawing a deep breath. 'If you are late, little cousin, then you are more than worth waiting for, believe me. May I get you a drink?'

She said with mock plaintiveness, 'Would you think me rude, Don Ramón, if I said I would rather have my dinner? I'm very hungry.'

Doña Isabella rose with a snakelike rustle of skirts. 'Then by all means let us go into dinner. It has been delayed long enough. Come, Pilar.'

She swept past Nicola, without a second glance, followed by her daughter.

Ramón said hurriedly, 'Nicola, I am truly sorry that Luis cannot be here tonight.'

She raised her eyebrows calmly. 'Why?'

'Well——' he spread his hands defensively, 'it is your first evening—your first dinner in your home. An auspicious occasion. You have every reason to complain about his absence.'

Nicola said, 'Don Luis' absences are something I shall have to get accustomed to. I may as well begin at once.' She had managed to say it without wincing, she thought, but she couldn't suppress the bitterness totally. 'Besides, I suppose there's something to admire in such—loyalty to an old friend.'

She had expected Ramón to faint with embarrassment and shock, but he registered nothing but surprise and dawning approbation.

He said, 'So you know—and you understand?'

'It seems I have little choice,' she said in a brittle voice. 'Now shall we go into dinner?'

And all through that interminable meal, she sat with Luis's pearl like a frozen tear between her breasts.

CHAPTER SIX

As her wedding day drew inexorably nearer, Nicola found the days were taking on a strangely dreamlike quality. She was very conscious that she was no longer in control of her own destiny, and as a consequence reality seemed to withdraw to a distance. But afterwards, certain incidents seemed to her to stand out with startling clarity.

She had spent quite some time writing letters—to her parents, to Elaine and to Teresita. The first had been incredibly difficult, because she had to leave so much unsaid. For instance, she could hardly write to two people who loved her, 'He makes me burst into flames if he so much as takes my hand, but he has a mistress in Santo Tomás a few miles away and he visits her several times a week, and will probably continue to do so after the wedding.' So instead she told them that she was very happy and that if they thought they could come to the wedding, Luis would send the air tickets immediately.

The letters to Elaine and Teresita were much easier, because she confined herself to a bald statement of the facts without explanation or expansion. Her sole concession was a 'Please don't worry about me' scrawled at the end of each.

Doña Isabella did not mellow as Luis had predicted, but her attitude gradually became more resigned as the wedding approached. Nicola suspected she derived a great deal of secret enjoyment from the arrangements in spite of her constant complaints. Certainly she made the most of playing the gracious hostess when visitors began arriving to meet Don Luis' *novia*. There were luncheon parties and supper parties, with guests from all over the state and beyond, some of them even arriving in their own private planes and helicopters on the landing strip at the rear of the *hacienda*. Nicola had discovered that Luis himself possessed a pilot's licence, and frequently took the controls at his own light aircraft which he kept at Monterrey airport.

Nicola found the frequent parties an ordeal, even when Luis was there at her side, and far worse when he was not. And he was not always there by any means. She was beginning to realise the extent of his wealth and responsibilities, and understand why he was often away at meetings, sometimes for days at a time.

She always felt uneasy when he was away from the *hacienda*. Not because she missed him, she assured herself swiftly, but because without his presence and protection she was always more aware of his family's hostility and disapproval.

Not Ramón, of course. If he had misgivings about his cousin's choice of bride, he concealed them well, and was always friendly and considerate, but he wasn't always there either, and it was then that his mother and sister began to plant their barbs, holding long conversations from which Nicola was excluded because she knew nothing of the people they were mentioning, or the incidents to which they referred. She knew they were deliberately showing her that she did not belong to their leisured world, and she wanted to say, 'Don't worry—it wasn't my idea. But the alternatives were pretty appalling too.'

She had sometimes wondered if she could appeal to Doña Isabella for help. The border with the United States couldn't be all that far away, but she guessed that if Doña Isabella had to weigh ridding herself of Nicola against deliberately arousing Luis' wrath, there would be no assistance there. Besides, Luis still had her passport, and during his absences, the door to his study was kept locked.

But her life wasn't just a constant stream of visitors

and social events. Señora Mendez, the dressmaker, was now installed at the *hacienda*, a small stout woman with flashing eyes and an imperious manner, trailing a downtrodden daughter carrying pattern books and fabric samples in her wake. Nicola was aware that the Señora was there to make her wedding dress, but she was frankly taken aback at the extent of the trousseau which was to be provided, particularly in view of the fact that there was to be no honeymoon trip as such. Luis had informed her abruptly that his business commitments were too pressing, but that he would arrange something later in the year.

'But if we're not going away, then I don't need all these clothes,' Nicola protested.

He lifted a brow, sending her a sardonic grin. 'I agree, *chica*, but we must not scandalise Tia Isabella.'

She had turned away, flushing, half in anger, and half with the forbidden excitement which always uncurled deep inside her when he looked at her like that. And it happened too often for comfort. Sometimes as she sat at the dining table, or on the terrace, or walked in the courtyard she would look up and see him watching her, a deep sensual hunger in his eyes which he made no effort to conceal.

In a way, although her mind rejected all the conventional connotations of a honeymoon, she felt it might have made things easier for her if they had gone away somewhere, if only for a few days. She would find it embarrassing in the extreme to have to face the small enclosed world of the *hacienda* each day as Luis's bride. But at the same time, it was impossible to confess her misgivings to Luis, to tell him frankly that she would prefer her transition from girlhood to womanhood to be observed by no other eyes but his.

Because that wasn't strictly true either. Each day, the implications of what she was about to do pressed more heavily upon her, filling her with a kind of panic. She might feel that she no longer had any real will of her own, that some unknown current was sweeping her away, and she could no longer swim against it, but the fact remained that the ultimate intimate submission still lay ahead of her, and she was terrified.

It was not just the thought of being alone with him which intimidated her, or of having to accede to demands which were still, in spite of any amount of theoretical enlightenment, very much a mystery. He had enough expertise, enough experience, she knew helplessly, to make it easy for her, to gentle her into acceptance of him—if he chose.

But instead he might simply choose to give free rein to the tightly leashed passion she sensed every time he came anywhere near her. After all, he had made no guarantees of consideration, or tenderness. He had said that he wanted her, and warned her not to fight him. And, worst of all, he knew that he could make her want him.

She had never dreamed it was possible to be so deeply, physically aware of another human being. And yet each time he returned to the *hacienda* from one of his trips, it was as if she was warned by some secret, invisible antennae. Long before she heard his voice, or recognised his long lithe stride, she knew when he was near her.

This was what frightened her—the prospect of total physical enslavement, the subjugation of her personality to his. If she was honest, it could already have taken place if he had made the slightest attempt to woo her, or even be alone with her. But he never did, and never had since that evening in her room when he had given her the pearl.

She had not worn the pearl since, although she had worn other jewellery he had given her—family heirlooms, most of them in exquisite if old-fashioned mountings.

And the best gift of all had been no heirloom, but barely more than a trinket, which he had handed to her quite casually one evening when they were all gathered in the *salón* before dinner. Inside the tissue wrappings of the small package, Nicola had found a butterfly, its body silver and its wings mother-of-pearl, to fasten in her hair. She had exclaimed in delight, turning to him with shining eyes as she tried to thank him, knowing that if only—if only they had been alone she would have cast restraint to the winds and kissed him. But she didn't dare, not as much as a swift peck on the cheek. He had shrugged, turning away. '*De nada*, Nicola. You seemed so intrigued with La Mariposa, I thought it might be appropriate.' Even a muttered comment from Pilar about 'cheap rubbish' had not dimmed her pleasure.

Although she had made a positive effort to establish some kind of relationship with Pilar, this had borne no fruit at all. The other girl avoided her whenever possible, and was inimical when they were in each other's company. Nicola was not convinced her behaviour was prompted by thwarted love for Luis either. She used no arts to allure him, to show him what he was missing. Her attitude wavered between bare civility and smouldering resentment, and in his turn Luis treated her with a guarded patience bordering on exasperation. Only the blind maternal love of someone like Doña Isabella could ever have linked them as a couple, Nicola decided ruefully.

As the days passed, the fact that she wasn't dreaming or that this whole situation was not some vast hideous joke being perpetrated on her in revenge began to come home to her fully. There were legal details to be settled, and papers to be signed, and she found herself obeying like an automaton, knowing as she did so that there was no turning back.

But did she even want to? If by some alchemy it was possible to wipe out the past weeks, to transform her into the girl she had been in Mexico City with nothing ahead of her but a sightseeing trip, would she do so?

I don't know, she thought. I just don't know. And

that, strangely, was the most disturbing thing of all.

From the niche above the altar, the painted eyes of the Virgin looked down. Nicola found her own gaze returning to the image time and time again as the ceremony which made her Luis' wife proceeded according to the time-honoured ritual. It was not so very different from the service which would have been held at home in England in the village church, as Father Gonzalo had explained during one of his visits in the past week to instruct her briefly in the Catholic faith.

But the church was very different—almost alien with its carving and gilding and the smell of incense heavy in the air, and the statue of the Mother of God was the most alien of all, in her heavy gold brocade robes stitched with precious stones, and the high gold coronet on her head. She was nothing like any of the smiling blue-robed Madonnas in English churches, Nicola thought. An honoured Christian symbol she might be, but at the same time there was something essentially pagan about the gorgeous robes, and the fixed almost inhuman smile, reminding Nicola, if she needed reminding, that the land they stood on had had Christianity imposed upon it, but that older, darker gods, worshipped in blood, still lingered in the memory of its people.

How many Montalba brides had those painted eyes watched? she wondered, as her voice obediently repeated the vows after Father Gonzalo. None of it seemed real, least of all herself in this dress—yard upon yard of billowing ivory silk—and the exquisite antique lace mantilla which Luis had asked her to wear. He did not explain, and she didn't ask, but there was something in the way he touched it as he handed it to her which told her it had been his mother's.

She wondered what her own mother would have thought if she had seen her like this. Her parents had wanted to come, but there was too much to do on the farm, so they had promised a visit later. 'When you're settled, darling,' her mother had written, and Nicola's lips had twisted ruefully at the homely phrase. It bore no relationship to any life she might expect to have with Luis.

But she had been surprised to learn that Luis had also written to them. He had never mentioned any such intention to her, and she had been pleased and a little touched by the gesture.

In the absence of her father, she had wondered who would give her away, until Luis's godfather had informed her during one of his visits that it would be his privilege to do so. He was a correct man, inclining towards stoutness, with a neat grey beard, and he was so like the mental image that Nicola had once harboured of Luis himself that she had had to fight to conceal a smile when she had first been introduced.

But he had been amazingly kind to her as he took her down the aisle on his arm, patting her hand reassuringly, and telling her that she was as beautiful as an angel.

Nicola didn't believe him, but she had been satisfied as she took a final look in her mirror. Señora Mendez was a genius, and her dress was wonderful, fairytale, dreamlike. And it would bring her good fortune, the Señora had smilingly assured her. Had she not sewn good luck tokens into the hem with her own hands?

'And there is also this.' With a droll look, she had slipped a flat tissue-wrapped parcel into Nicola's hands. 'Always for my brides I do this. One gown for the day, and another for the night.' She sighed sentimentally, gave Nicola's skirt one last professional twitch, and departed.

Nicola undid the white ribbon and unfolded the tissue, knowing what she would find. It was a nightdress, white as a cloud in chiffon, falling from the tiniest of bodices in handmade lace. Nicola stared at it, feeling panic rising in her throat again.

'Ah, how beautiful!' Maria who was hovering nearby,

darted forward. 'Let me take it, *señorita*. See?' She allowed the material to drift across her hand and arm so that Nicola could see just how sheer and transparent the wretched garment was.

Maria sent her an arch look, began to say something, then thought better of it.

Nicola wrenched her thoughts back to the present, aware of a frozen feeling in her throat, as Luis' ring slid into place on her finger. She was married—married twice, in fact, because earlier in the cool of the morning they had driven to Santo Tomás for a brief civil ceremony.

The evening before, she had chosen a moment when she knew Luis was in his study and alone and had gone to him there.

He had risen as soon as she appeared hesitantly in the doorway, his brows lifting in surprise.

'You honour me, *querida*. I had imagined you busied with a thousand last-minute details.'

'No,' she said. 'There's nothing. Your aunt is very efficient. Everything is ready—except . . .' She hesitated.

'Except?' he prompted.

'Except myself,' she said wretchedly. 'Luis, it still isn't too late. You could let me go.'

He came round the desk to her side, his eyes narrowed, and the dark brows drawn together in a swift frown.

'What nonsense is this?'

'It isn't nonsense,' she protested. 'You can't marry me—you know you can't. Why don't you just—allow me to leave? There might be talk at first, but Doña Isabella would soon convince everyone you'd had a lucky escape.'

He shook his head. 'There will be no talk, because you are not leaving. How could you, anyway, without this?' He reached behind him and picked up her passport which had been lying on the desk. He opened the cover and looked down at it. 'I see I am required to allow the

bearer to pass freely, and without "let or hindrance." '
He smiled faintly. 'Much as I respect your Queen, I have
no intention of obeying this request.' He slipped the
passport into his pocket. 'This stays with me, *amiga*,
and so do you.'

She went on looking at him. 'Oh God, why are you
doing this?' she asked raggedly. 'What do you want from
me?'

His voice was silky 'I want a wife, Nicola. And I want
a son. You will give me both. You forced your way into
my life. Now you will remain there—always.'

She said tonelessly, 'For the last time, Luis—please
let me go.'

Mockingly he shook his head. '*Jamas*, *amante*.
Never.'

She left him without another word, and went straight
to her room. That morning in the car on the way to
Santo Tomás they had sat like strangers, without a
word. In fact she wasn't sure if he'd even looked at her
properly until much later, as she came into the chapel
on his godfather's arm. All the way to the altar, he had
watched her with arrogant possession in his eyes.

Now Father Gonzalo was pronouncing a final blessing, and Luis was helping her up from her knees. His
eyes were enigmatic as they met hers, and her own
glance slid nervously away.

People were smiling and bowing to her as she moved
with her bridegroom towards the open doors and the
sunlight. Many of them were now familiar faces from
previous visits to the *hacienda*, and Nicola forced herself
to respond to the greetings, pretend to be the happy
bride they all expected.

Yet there was one face that was not in the slightest
degree familiar. Nicola noticed it at once, because she
knew she would not have forgotten if she had ever met
such an outstandingly beautiful woman. Her jet black
hair was drawn severely back into a chignon, and she
was exquisitely dressed and made up, her heavy lidded

eyes and full-lipped mouth being particularly accentuated.

Then they were outside in the late sunlight, and there were others crowding round, the *peons* who worked in the fields, the *vaqueros* who rode with the cattle, the servants, all offering their congratulations.

The religious ceremony had been held after the hour of siesta, because it would be followed by a party. Soon there would be music in the courtyard, as she had once imagined, and dancing and the inevitable fireworks. All the hallmarks of a celebration, and she, who was the centre of all these festivities, felt as if she was dying inside.

Presently she would be expected to dance, and to dance with Luis. Everyone, she supposed, would want to dance with the bride, but he was her husband, so it was his right. She didn't want to think about those other rights which he would demand later, much later, when the music had stopped. Perhaps she could bribe the musicians, she thought, to play and play all that night, and through the following day and the one after that . . . She caught at herself as a little bubble of sheer hysteria rose within her.

Inside the house Carlos, all smiles, was opening wine—imported vintage champagne. Nicola took the glass she was offered and sipped, still with that mechanical smile on her lips.

Doña Isabella and Pilar came and embraced her, their cheeks brushing hers swiftly and formally before they stepped away, their duty done. Ramón kissed her hand and whispered, 'Luis is the most fortunate of men.'

She went on smiling until she thought her face would crack into a thousand little pieces as the guests filed past to utter their congratulations. So much good will, so many good wishes, and yet she could believe in none of it. It was all still part of the charade she had begun back in Mexico City. She was like a puppet, dressed in garments which didn't belong to her, and manipulated by strangers. But all too soon there was coming a time when the doll would change into a woman. She might have come to this place as a counterfeit bride, but tonight Luis would exact full recompense from her in a currency which was only too real.

Suddenly she knew she had to escape from the smiles, the torrent of words, and the knowing looks.

She turned to Luis. 'The mantilla is making my head ache. May I remove it before the dancing?'

'Of course.' He studied her pale face frowningly. 'Shall I send Maria to you?'

'Oh, no, I can manage,' she said hastily.

The quiet room upstairs was no longer hers alone. The bed had been re-made, she saw at once, with lace-edged sheets and extra pillows, and Señora Mendez' nightgown was laid across the foot of it like a cloud of foam.

Nicola removed the pins which held the mantilla, working carefully to avoid tearing the delicate lace, then started violently as a knock came at the door.

It was Carmela, smiling broadly. 'This letter came for you, *señora*. Señor Don Luis said I should give it to you at once.'

Nicola took it wonderingly, her brow clearing as she recognised her mother's handwriting. It was just a note, brief but full of love, to tell her that they would all be thinking of her, and sending affectionate messages to Luis that she would never dare pass on, because it was her fault that they believed that this was a conventional marriage, and that they were getting a son-in-law who would value such sentiments.

There was also a postscript. 'I'm enclosing this letter which came for you the other day from Switzerland. I think it's probably from Tess. Did you manage to keep in touch with her?'

The short answer to that was no, Nicola thought wryly. She had avoided writing to any of her Zurich friends in case they inadvertently included news of Ewan which she didn't want to hear, although most of them knew what had happened.

She glanced at the other envelope, then slipped it into a drawer. She would read it later.

It was getting darker outside, and out in the courtyard she could hear the sound of musicians tuning up. The dancing couldn't start without her, so it was time she went down.

Luis advanced to meet her, an elegant stranger in his black suit, its short jacket embroidered in silver. Nicola let him take her cold hand in his, and put his arm round her waist. She had been frightened that she might go to pieces altogether when he touched her, but his clasp was too light and formal for that. At any other time, she might have enjoyed moving with him in a swift waltz round the circle of smiling faces, while they applauded and showered them with flower petals. Her dress billowed out as he swung her round, and then it was over, and someone else was eagerly claiming her hand, and she was whirled away. She caught a glimpse of him over her new partner's shoulder, and saw that he was smiling faintly. He could afford to smile, she thought, because he knew however many men she might dance with, in the end she would be alone with him. Wherever she went and whoever she danced with, his glance seemed to find her. He was the hawk of her nightmare, she thought, hovering, knowing his prey is there for the taking.

She ate food she did not want, replied to questions she barely heard, and eventually turned to a touch on her arm to find Pilar confronting her.

'Nicola.' Her smile was sugary. 'There is someone here who so much wishes to meet you. May I present the Señora Doña Carlota Garcia?'

It was the woman she had noticed in the chapel. In close-up she was even more striking, Nicola thought numbly, and her dark red dress was exquisitely cut to

draw attention to her slim waist and full voluptuous
breasts.

Her voice was low and charming. 'It is a pleasure to
meet you, Doña Nicola. I would have called before, but
since my husband's death I have myself become deeply
involved in politics, and I travel a good deal. But I
would not miss the wedding of such an old friend as
Luis for anything in the world.'

A number of replies occurred to Nicola, but a glance
at the spiteful triumph in Pilar's face kept her silent.

She said at last, slowly, 'It is a—pleasure for me also,
señora. I have heard a great deal about you.'

Señora Garcia laughed, displaying perfect teeth. 'Not
from Luis, I hope! We know each other so well that he
is hardly a reliable informant. He flatters me too much.'

Nicola raised her eyebrows coolly. 'I don't think Luis
has ever mentioned you to me. No, it was someone else
who spoke of you.'

Señora Garcia looked slightly disconcerted, she was
pleased to note. 'I—see. Well, I hope we can be friends.'
She gave Nicola another smile and walked away,
followed by Pilar.

And I, Nicola silently addressed her departing back,
hope we never meet again. She was surprised how angry
the unexpected encounter had made her, but told herself
defensively that it was not the fact that Luis had a mistress—for all she knew he had half a dozen—but that
he had had the unmitigated gall to invite her to his
wedding. But then he had no reason to believe that his
bride even suspected her existence, she thought.

'You look cross, little cousin. Has some clumsy fool
stamped on your foot?' Ramón had suddenly materialised at her side, and beyond him she could see Luis
advancing through the crowd.

She smiled swiftly. 'It's nothing. Dance with me,
Ramón.'

He looked taken aback. 'But Luis . . .'

'Oh, he won't lack for partners, and you've hardly

been near me all evening,' she protested with almost a pout. She put out a hand and traced some of the embroidery on his sleeve. 'I shall begin to think you dislike me as much as your mother and sister do.'

'*Nombre de Dios*,' Ramón muttered, looking suddenly anguished. 'They do not—I do not—I—oh, very well, let us dance.'

Luis had stopped and was watching them, she knew, and quite deliberately she allowed her hand to slide from Ramón's shoulder towards his collar, smiling radiantly into his face as she did so.

He looked as if he was about to have a heart attack. 'Nicola, I beg of you! Is this some game? I warn you, it is a dangerous one. Luis is my cousin and my friend, but his anger can be formidable.'

'But you're a wonderful dancer, Ramón.' She looked at him through her lashes. 'I am sure my—husband wouldn't grudge me these few minutes of pleasure at my own party.'

'If you think that, then you do not know him at all,' Ramón said bluntly. 'Let me take you to him, Nicola. Please do not provoke him further.'

'Spoilsport!' She pulled a face at him. 'Very well, if you're so frightened of him.'

'I am more frightened for you than for myself. Do you wish to begin your married life with a beating at his hands?'

'He wouldn't dare,' she said defiantly.

He gave her a despairing look. 'If you believe that, then you are—forgive me—a fool. Anyway, the dancing will end soon. It is nearly time for the firework display, and when that starts it is the custom in our family for the bride to—to retire.'

'I've no intention of doing anything of the sort. I want to see the fireworks. This is supposed to be my party, and I shall enjoy every last minute of it,' Nicola said coolly. 'Customs like that belong to history, not the present day, anyway.'

Ramón's pleasant mouth set in a line which indicated that he would not be averse to starting off the prescribed beating with a box on the ears on his own account.

In a carefully neutral tone, he said, 'That is an argument which should more properly be directed to your husband, my cousin, *señora*. I will take you to him.'

Luis was lounging against one of the pillars of the terrace, glass in hand, as they approached. He straightened and smiled, but the smile did not reach his eyes.

Ramón said, 'I have brought you your errant bride, *amigo*. It seems she does not care for some of our customs.' He took Nicola's hand from his arm and placed it firmly in that of Luis before moving off.

Luis raised her hand to his lips. To a casual onlooker it would have been a charming, gallant gesture, but then a casual onlooker would not have seen the cold rage in his eyes.

He said, 'And which of our conventions do you wish to flout now, *chica*?'

Her heart thudding painfully, Nicola said, 'Ramón told me that I would be expected to leave before the fireworks display. He said it was a family custom—but I don't see why I should do so.'

He shrugged. 'Stay, then. It was designed originally to spare the blushes of the bride, I believe, but no one who has witnessed your conduct tonight, clinging round my cousin's neck like a *puta*, would believe you had any blushes to spare.'

He let her hand fall and walked away, leaving her standing there, the colour fading from her cheeks. Out of the corner of her eye she could see curious glances being cast at her, some of them slightly censorious, and, what was worse, Doña Isabella bearing down on her, bristling with self-righteousness. Nicola took a deep breath, picked up her skirts and fled through the laughing, chattering groups, along the terrace and into the house.

Maria was waiting in her room. Nicola allowed her

to unhook the wedding dress and take it away, and then to the girl's obvious chagrin told her that she could go.

From the noise of explosions, the flashes of light and colour, she guessed the fireworks had begun. She could hear laughter and applause as she sat in her long waist slip and scrap of a bra and looked at herself defeatedly. Luis didn't need to beat her, she thought. He could take the skin from her by his tone of voice alone. And she had stood there like a fool. Why hadn't she accused him in turn?

Furiously she blinked back the tears which for some unaccountable reason were pricking at her eyelids. Soon, when the display was over, those guests who were not being accommodated overnight in the guest wing would be leaving. Luis would say goodbye to them as a courteous host, and then, angry or not, he would come to her room. She didn't want to be found skulking at the dressing table in her undies.

Quickly she undressed and showered, then reluctantly donned the exquisite nightdress waiting for her. She brushed her hair, then on an impulse looked in her jewellery case and pinned the silver butterfly among the tawny silk strands.

She was just going to close the drawer when she saw the letter her mother had sent on. She wasn't in the mood for Tess's usual brand of cheerful chat, but on the other hand she didn't want to sit here, waiting for Luis and becoming twitchier by the moment, so she tore open the envelope and extracted the thin sheet of paper inside. The envelope had been typewritten, but she knew the writing on the letter as soon as she saw it. It was Ewan's.

She felt sick suddenly. Ewan writing to her? It couldn't be possible! She unfolded the paper and began to read, her heart thumping slowly and painfully.

'My dearest Nicola,' she read, 'I expect I'm the last person you ever thought to hear from again. After the things we said before we parted, I'm amazed I have the

guts to write to you at all, but I can't stop thinking
about you, and all we meant to each other once.

'You probably don't know that I've been a widower
for over six months. Greta was killed in a road accident.
Her car skidded on some ice and went out of control on
a bend. It was a shock, naturally, but I won't pretend it
was the end of the world for me. Frankly, our marriage
wasn't working out, and we'd discussed separation just
before she had the accident. You know how fast she
always used to drive. I always thought it was out of
character, as she was quite a stick-in-the-mud in other
ways.

'I was a fool to let you go—I've known that for a
long time. I'm beginning to get my life together again
now, and I want you back in it. I know I treated you
badly, darling. Forgive me, and tell me that we can start
again. Don't let one mistake ruin both our lives a second
time. The way you used to feel about me, there must be
something left in spite of all the hurt. Write to me,
Nicky. Tell me you love me still. I need you. All my
love, darling, Ewan.'

Nicola sat stunned, the words dancing crazily in front
of her eyes. Ewan—Greta—could it be true? Breathing
shakily, she read the letter again, then crumpled it into
a ball and thrust it back into the drawer which she
slammed shut.

She looked at her white-faced image in the mirror.
Ewan, she thought incredulously. Ewan was free and
wanted her. And life had played her its cruellest trick of
all by allowing her to know this tonight of all nights.
Her stifled laugh sounded like a sob, and she lifted her
hands to her head, trying to get her thoughts into some
kind of coherent order.

But Ewan—Zurich—everything that had happened
there between them seemed light years away, like a half-
remembered dream.

Ewan, she thought. Ewan, whom she loved, and who
had hurt her so that she would never love again.

Desperately she tried to conjure his face up in her mind. Brown hair, curling slightly, blue eyes always smiling, a deep cleft in his chin, she thought feverishly. But that wasn't the image that she saw. The man in her imagination was as dark as night itself, the planes and angles of his face, harshly carved, with strength and pride in its lines. And his eyes did not smile, but looked at her with bitter scorn.

Oh God! She got up from the dressing stool and began to walk round the room, her hands pressed to suddenly heated cheeks. What did it all mean? Ewan had been her love, her only love. He had broken her heart. How could she have forgotten so soon?

The answer was a sombre one. Because Luis had made her forget. From the moment she had met him, he had occupied her thoughts to the exclusion of everything else. Each time he had kissed her, and God knew they had been few enough, each caress had been indelibly printed on her memory, making her ache with longing. Ewan hadn't been able to awaken half the dormant passion which the first brush of Luis' mouth on hers had brought searingly to life.

Her appalling behaviour downstairs, turning her back on him to dance with his cousin, hadn't been because she fancied Ramón even for a moment, or because she wanted to establish herself as an independent spirit, untrammelled by outworn conventions, but because she had been so blazingly jealous of Carlota Garcia.

All the time she had been dancing with Ramón, driving him near to a nervous breakdown with her come-hither looks, she had been seeing Luis with Carlota, imagining them making love, and the pain had been almost more than she could bear.

She had wanted to hurt Luis, and she had only succeeded in hurting herself, because he didn't care. He wanted her—he had never made any secret of it. He wanted her to give him children, and he would expect conduct from her befitting his wife, but nothing else.

And tonight when he touched her at last, and she turned to starlight and flame in his arms, he would know beyond doubt what she herself had only just come to realise—that she loved him.

She shivered, wrapping her arms round her body. It had been there in her mind for so long, unacknowledged, that it was almost a relief to admit it at last. She had fought it from the beginning, labelling it as a sheer physical attraction, but she had lost.

Now she could confess to herself how empty her life had seemed every time Luis had gone away, and how eagerly she had waited for his return. She had never shown it, of course, and she still could not, because nothing had changed.

He was marrying because he desired her, and that was all. If she hadn't appealed to him sexually, then she would probably be in jail at this moment. As it was, he had decided on some whim to create his own intimate prison for her.

And this room was to be her cell. She lifted her head and stared round her. It was quiet now, the sounds of revelry fading from the courtyard beneath. She would not be alone for very much longer. Did she have the strength to pretend the indifference she had threatened? Could she endure to have Luis only as her lover when the truth was that she wanted him as her love?

She stood, pressing one fist against her lips like a bewildered child, wondering what to do. There was nowhere to run, nowhere to hide, not even from herself.

But in spite of her inner agony, she was becoming slowly aware of something else. Not far away, there was music, softly played on guitars, and someone singing in a warm baritone. She went over to the window and peeped round the shutter. They stood in a semi-circle in the courtyard below, looking up towards the window, a group of *mariachi* serenaders, probably from Santo Tomás. Hidden by the shutter, she stood and listened, a wistful smile touching the corner of her mouth. Once he had sent them away, but they were here tonight probably because it was yet another custom.

Nicola wasn't sure when she first realised that she was no longer alone in the bedroom, but she didn't turn immediately because she could use the song as an excuse.

Finally it ended, and the guitars took up another melody, sweet and sensuous, and slowly she turned and looked at him. He was standing only a few feet away from her, wearing a dressing gown in some dark silk, and nothing else, she was certain, because the robe was open to the waist and his legs were bare.

He was looking at her as if the sight of her had turned him to stone, and with a sudden surge of shyness she realised what he was seeing—the gleam of her body through the film of chiffon, her small high breasts cupped but not concealed by the tiny lace bodice. She wanted to speak, but no words would come.

He said huskily, 'Skin like ivory, and hair like gold. *Alma de mi vida,* do you know how beautiful you are?'

The sensual hunger in his eyes was a devastation, and every fibre in her responded to it in a great blaze of yearning. More than life itself she wanted to take the few steps into his arms. But if she did, she would be betrayed utterly, and she panicked, stepping backwards, lifting her hands as if to ward him off.

Yet he had not moved—and nor did he, for one long moment. She saw that fierce desire fading from his face, to be replaced fleetingly by incredulity, and then an immense weariness as he turned away and walked towards the bed, untying the belt of his robe as he went.

Realising that she was right about his nakedness, Nicola averted her gaze hastily. When she did venture to look towards the bed, Luis was in it, safely covered by the sheet, staring up at the ceiling with his arms folded behind his head.

He said at last on a note of polite interest, 'Do you intend to stand there all night?'

'Yes—no—I don't know,' she stammered feeling more of a fool and worse than a fool with every second that passed.

'Then I advise you to make up your mind,' he said. There was a pause, then he added expressionlessly, 'Unless you wish me to make the decision for you by forcing you?'

Appalled, she gasped, 'No!'

He turned his head on the pillow and looked at her coolly. 'It is what you seem to expect. A moment ago you looked at me with terror in your eyes. I did not enjoy the experience, which is a new one to me, I confess.'

'I'm—sorry,' she said inadequately. 'But—but you're not making this very easy for me.'

'Perhaps because I do not fully understand the difficulty. You have shared a bed with me before, or had you forgotten?'

'No.' She shook her head. 'But that was different.'

'How so?' He sounded faintly bored.

Nicola hesitated. To say 'Well, for one thing you had your clothes on,' was going to sound ludicrously prim and schoolgirlish, and besides that, hadn't she secretly speculated a dozen times or more on what he would look like without them?

Instead she said, 'I—I wasn't your wife then,' which was hardly any better.

His voice was cold. 'Nor are you now, either in body, or in your stubborn little mind, *amiga*. A few words said over us does not make a marriage. Or did you think that after all I would be content to admire you at a distance?'

'No,' she shook her head again, feeling totally ridiculous. 'You made it clear you wanted—children.'

He turned on to his side, supporting himself on an elbow, a brief crooked smile touching his mouth. 'Eventually, yes. But you are deluding yourself if you think I want you here in my arms simply to make you pregnant. You do not really believe that?'

Huskily, she said, 'No.'

'*Muy bien.*' He reached over and threw back the sheet on the other side of the bed. 'Then join me, *querida, por favor*,' he added mockingly.

Nicola walked across the room as slowly as she dared, and slid under the turned-back sheet, lying rigidly on the very edge of the bed. There was a click and the big lamp beside the bed was extinguished, plunging the room into darkness.

Nicola scarcely breathed, waiting tensely for—what? A kiss, a touch, the removal of her nightgown, all or any of them.

'You see?' Luis said silkily. 'It was not as impssible as you thought. Sleep well, *querida*. I am glad for your sake that the bed is so wide. A metre or so less and there might have been a chance of my brushing against you accidentally in the night. As it is, you can cower there with your virginal fears in perfect safety. *Buenas noches.*'

Endless seconds spun themselves into an eternity of minutes as Nicola lay, staring into the darkness. Her heart thudding she said at last, 'Luis . . .' her voice low and tentative.

'*Si?*' His tone was not encouraging, and he actually sounded drowsy, she thought incredulously.

Taking her courage by the scruff of the neck, she ventured, 'If you want me . . .'

'You do me too much honour, *amiga*, but no. I have as little taste for rape as yourself. And don't forget you made me very angry earlier. Be grateful for your reprieve, and go to sleep.'

The humiliation of it made her shrink, while the space between them yawned as wide and unfathomable as an ocean.

But how could she explain to him—ever—that it was not the act of love she feared, but the unwanted emotions she might betray while she was in his arms?

Meanwhile her body ached for fulfilment, and she turned her head miserably, seeking a cool place on the pillow. Luis wanted her: she knew it. Perhaps he was waiting for her to make the next move. What if she turned towards him, touched him, let her hand slide from his shoulder down his arm to his hip . . .

And what if he told her to go to sleep again? she asked herself bitterly. Could she face another bleak rejection?

She was still debating the point when exhaustion finally dragged her into a fitful and troubled sleep.

CHAPTER SEVEN

IT was late when she awoke. Maria was standing beside the bed, holding a breakfast tray, and smiling selfconsciously.

'*Buenos dias, señora.*' As Nicola sat up dazedly, she seized her pillows and plumped them up for her to lean against before placing the tray across her lap. 'It is a beautiful morning, *señora.*'

Nicola gave a wry glance at the bright sunlight spilling across the floor. 'I think it's more like afternoon, Maria.'

'Perhaps,' Maria shrugged. 'What does it matter? The Señor Don Luis gave orders that we were not to disturb you earlier.' She giggled. 'Also he sends you this,' she added triumphantly, pointing to a single red rose in a small crystal vase in the centre of the tray.

Nicola stared at it, completely at a loss. 'How kind of him,' she remarked at last.

Maria gasped. 'Kind? Ah, no, *señora.* You do not understand. It is a local custom.'

'Another of them,' Nicola muttered, but Maria went chattering on.

'Here, when the wedding night is over, the husband sends his wife a flower as a token of how she has pleased him. And the Señor Don Luis sends you a red rose, *señora*, the flower of love itself.' She giggled again. 'He must be a happy man this morning!'

The Señor Don Luis, Nicola thought savagely, was a cynical, sarcastic bastard. She pushed the tray away.

'I'm not hungry, Maria. I want to get dressed.'

'But, *señora,*' Maria's eyes nearly popped out of her head, 'should you not—remain where you are?'

131

Nicola felt a slight flush rise in her cheeks. She said, 'No, Maria. Run me a bath, please, and I'll wear the green dress.'

'*Ay de mi!*' Maria lamented. She did as she was told, but her expression said plainly that any woman fortunate to be sent a red rose after a night of passion with Don Luis should lie back and wait for further goodies to come her way.

She looked reasonable, Nicola thought, as she gave herself a last critical look in the mirror. A little shadowy under the eyes, but that would be expected, she thought ironically.

She was on her way to the door when Maria's shocked voice halted her. '*Señora*—your flower!' She was holding out the rose.

Nicola stared at it. 'What am I supposed to do with it?' she asked flatly.

Maria gestured almost despairingly. 'Wear it in your hair, *señora*. Or carry it, or pin it to your dress against your heart.'

'I'll carry it,' Nicola decided with ill grace, but she was beginning to wonder whether the rose had been presented to her with quite the irony she had at first thought. She hadn't realised it was a token she would be expected to exhibit publicly, but now she could see that in its way, the flower was a chivalrous gesture on Luis' part. After last night's fiasco, he could have sent nothing at all, or the Mexican equivalent of bindweed, and given the whole household something to whisper about in corners. Whereas now, everyone would think that the *dueño* was well pleased with his bride.

She looked down at the rose with sudden tears in her eyes. And it could have been true, she thought fiercely, if only she hadn't been such a fool.

As she walked slowly towards the stairs, nerving herself for the ordeal by curiosity ahead, she wondered wistfully how differently the day might have begun for her if Luis and she had been lovers. She might have been kissed awake in his arms instead of finding herself alone, she thought, and sighed.

As she reached the foot of the stairs, Pilar came into the hall from the *salón* and stood staring at her.

'*Buenos dias.*' Her lips curled unpleasantly. '*Pobrecita*, I suppose you are searching for your bridegroom. How sad for you that his ardour cooled so quickly, and what a pity for him that he didn't come to his senses sooner.'

'I can't think what you mean,' Nicola said coolly.

'No? When the whole world knows how early he left your room this morning, driven away by your English coldness, no doubt.'

Nicola suppressed a wince, then deliberately she lifted the rose which had been hidden by the folds of her skirt and brushed it almost casually across her lips.

Pilar's eyes widened incredulously, then, with a noise like a kitten which has just received an unexpected boot in the midriff, she flounced away.

Nicola was still standing rather hesitantly at the foot of the stairs when Carlos appeared carrying a tray of glasses. He gave her a respectful bow and a smile, and was disappearing towards the *comedor* when she called him back.

'Carlos, do you know where—my husband is?'

'I think Don Luis is at the stables, *señora*. Shall I have a message sent to him?'

'Oh no,' she said quickly. 'I'll go and find him myself.'

'As you wish, Doña Nicola.'

Luis was standing talking to Juan Hernandez as she approached, and they both turned and looked at her. Luis smiled, but his eyes were hooded and enigmatic, and she felt herself blush faintly.

He said, 'I was about to request you to join me, *mi amada*. I have something to show you.'

In some bewilderment she followed him to one of the stalls. Juan Hernandez whisked inside and Nicola heard him murmuring caressingly in his own language and clicking his tongue. When he reappeared he was leading one of the prettiest mares Nicola had ever seen, chestnut with a star on her forehead. She gasped in delight.

'Oh, she's beautiful!'

'I am glad she pleases you, *querida*.' Luis' voice was laconic. 'She only arrived earlier this morning, so she will need a day or two to get used to her new home— and for Juan to make sure she has no hidden vices. Although it seems unlikely,' he added, running his hand down the satin neck.

Nicola made herself meet his eyes. 'You mean—she's for me?'

'For no one else,' he drawled. 'Her name is Estrella.'

Juan Hernandez had tactfully vanished. Nicola said, 'I—I don't know how to thank you.'

'Don't you, *amiga*?' His smile slanted mockingly. 'Perhaps we had better postpone any discussion of that to another occasion.'

Her flush deepened hectically, but before she could think of a reply, he had turned away and was putting Estrella back in her stall.

As Luis rejoined her, she said quickly, 'I also have to thank you for this.' She held out the rose.

He gave it a casual look and shrugged. *'De nada.* I suppose Maria told you its significance.'

'Yes, she did.' Nicola bit her lip. 'It was—kind of you.' She gave a little uneven laugh. 'It's already saved me from some unpleasant remarks from your cousin Pilar.'

His mouth tightened. 'That girl needs a good hiding— or something to do with her time. I blame myself. At one time she was keen to go to university, but her mother set up such scenes, such weeping and lamentations at the idea that I allowed myself to be persuaded against it.'

'But why?'

He gave her a dry look. 'Tia Isabella belongs to a school of thought which believes that women should be trained solely in the domestic virtues. She sees education as the cause of all the ills in our world. And she believed that if she kept Pilar at La Mariposa and thrust her at me continually, I would eventually ask her to be my wife. She has fixed but mistaken views on the value of proximity,' he added drily.

'But you could have overridden your aunt, surely.'

'Yes—but I had my own doubts about Pilar's wish to go to university. At the time she was very much under an influence which I found undesirable.'

Nicola stared at the ground. 'It might have solved a lot of problems if you'd married her. Why didn't you?'

'You have a poor memory, *querida*. Only yesterday I married you.'

'Yes—but when you decided to marry me, it was because you wanted a wife, not me particularly. I mean, you were prepared to marry Teresita whom you hardly knew, because your families wanted it—so why not Pilar?'

He said, 'The only time I have been tempted to lay a hand on my cousin Pilar is when I have also been holding my riding whip. Teresita was at least well-mannered and docile. After marriage she would probably have wearied me with her devotion, but she would have created no problems.'

Wearied me with her devotion. The words were like a knife in Nicola's heart.

'You were really going to marry her,' she said slowly. 'And yet losing her hasn't cost you a single sleepless night.'

'Why waste a sleepless night on a woman who is absent?' he asked mockingly. 'And I must correct you, *chica*. If I'd wanted any wife, I could have married a dozen times over. I married you because I wanted you, Nicola. I was angry at the trick you attempted to play on my family, but at the same time I could not help admiring your audacity and being amused by it. As our journey together proceeded, I began to realise that some of the assumptions I had made about you were untrue. Your reactions to me showed plainly that you were still a virgin, which I had not expected. It was then that I decided to make you my wife instead of my mistress.'

'So really the choice you offered was no choice at all.' She paused. 'What if I'd stuck to my guns and refused to marry you?'

He laughed. 'Then I would have spent a long and enjoyable night persuading you to change your mind.'

She said in a low voice, 'Then what makes—that night so different from last night?'

The amusement died sharply from his face. He said, 'Because at the *ejido*, although you were apprehensive, you did not look at me as if I were your executioner.'

Nicola flushed painfully. 'I'm sorry,' she said in a constricted tone.

'And so am I,' Luis said wryly. 'I am not accustomed to being regarded by a woman as if I was a monster, nor having her cringe away from me in sheer terror. But as for the sake of appearances, at least, we should continue to share a room for a few weeks, it is something I must learn to live with.'

Her heart began to thud slowly and uncomfortably. She did not look at him.

'You mean—you're not going to . . .'

'That is precisely what I mean. I have never forced myself on an unwilling woman in my life, and I do not intend to begin with you. Don't look so troubled, *querida*,' he added harshly. 'I shall come to your room after you are asleep, and leave before you wake. You will be disturbed as little as possible.'

She moved her shoulders helplessly. 'I don't understand—one minute you say you want me—and now . . .'

'Oh, I still want you, *querida*, make no mistake about that. But I shall not take you. Or did you imagine my lust was so great that I would be prepared to pursue my own gratification while you lay there—and thought of England, as I believe your saying is? *Muchas gracias, señora.* I prefer to wait in the hope that some time you will come to me willingly.' He paused. 'In the past you've used words like "hatred" and "repulsion" to me. I told myself you did not mean them, but after what I saw in your face last night, I am no longer sure.'

But I didn't mean them, she thought in agony, and if you said one word of love to me, I'd throw myself at your feet.'

Aloud she said woodenly, 'You are very generous, *señor*. Shall—shall I see you at lunch?'

'Of course. As far as the household is concerned, we shall lead a normal life together—and we still have guests.' He gave her a long cool look. 'It would be wiser to give them no more cause for gossip.'

She said, 'Yes, I understand,' and left him.

She was halfway back to the house before she noticed the blood on her hand. She unclenched her fist, and found one last unsuspected thorn left on her rose. As she stood in the sunlight, she felt tears on her face.

She felt limp with exhaustion by the time of the *siesta*. Playing the part of the happy bride was not easy when she felt as if she was cracking apart, and matters were not improved by Luis' effortless assumption of the role of devoted and attentive groom. Under the approving gaze of everyone at the *hacienda*, with the notable exceptions of his aunt and Pilar, he hardly stirred from her side, his arm curving possessively round her slim waist, brushing his mouth gently against her cheek or the lobe of her ear, or holding her hand and pressing lingering kisses to each finger in turn.

Nicola burned, and not solely from embarrassment. She was thankful that she was able to look shyly away, and not meet the mockery in his eyes.

Safe at last in her room, she leaned against the panels of the door for a moment, drawing a deep breath, hardly able to believe that she had escaped at last from the indulgent smiles downstairs that said without words that all the world loved a lover.

If they only knew, she thought drearily. She shed her clothes and had a long, relaxing shower before wrapping herself in her thinnest robe and coming back to the bedroom to collapse on the bed in the shuttered half-light.

The opening door was the last thing she expected, and she sat up, propping herself on her elbow and staring in open alarm as Luis came in carrying a bottle of wine and two glasses.

She stammered, 'You—what are you doing here?'

Her evident apprehension made him smile cynically. 'Don't worry, *querida*. I am simply fulfilling the expectations of our well-wishers by spending the *siesta* in the arms of my loving wife. Or that's what they are supposed to think. The truth will remain our secret. Would you like some wine?'

'No.'

'As you wish.' Deftly he opened the bottle and poured some into his own glass. 'Now, shall we remain here in silence and contemplate what might have been, or shall we talk?' There was a chaise-longue near the window, and he stretched out on that.

Nicola said reluctantly, 'Talk, I suppose.'

'A wise choice,' he said drily. 'Will you choose the topic?'

'Very well.' Her heart began to thump. 'Why don't we discuss—politics?'

Luis looked at her in amazement. 'Are you interested in politics?'

'I'm sure I could be,' she said. 'After all, you find them fascinating, don't you?'

'Do I, *amiga*? What has given you that idea, I wonder?'

She backtracked hurriedly. 'Well, a lot of your friends are politicians.'

'I have friends in a great many walks of life. I wasn't aware of a bias towards politics.'

She wanted to face him, to say bluntly, 'What about

Carlota Garcia?' But she couldn't bring herself to frame the words. She felt too vulnerable. And besides, questions of that nature might lead him to deduce that she was jealous, with everything that implied. It was better, she thought unhappily, to leave well alone.

She said like a polite child, 'I'm sorry, I must have made a mistake.'

'You seem to make a great many.' There was an edge to his voice. 'But while we are on the subject, my godfather has informed me that there has been further agitation over land reform to the east of here, so you will oblige me, when Estrella is ready for you, by not riding anywhere alone. If Juan Hernandez is not free to accompany you, then one of the grooms must do so. Do I make myself clear?'

'Perfectly clear.' She paused. 'Is—your friend—the man you used to know involved in this?'

'Not directly, perhaps.' Luis said briefly. 'But like many idealists he is now finding it is much easier to begin something than to control it once it is under way. Compared with some of his disciples, he is now almost a moderate. An irony, certainly.'

'Where is he?' asked Nicola.

He shrugged, drinking some of his wine. 'In hiding somewhere.' He sent her a sardonic look. 'You seem to be taking a close interest in him, *querida*. Does the thought of an outlaw's life appeal to the romance in your soul?'

No, she thought. You appeal to me—physically, mentally, in every way there is. You and you alone.

She traced some of the embroidery on the coverlet with her finger. 'Perhaps.'

'Then at least you and my cousin Pilar have something in common,' Luis said, and rose abruptly, and began to unfasten his shirt. 'You'd better close your virginal eyes, *amiga*. I'm going to take a shower.'

Nicola lay listening to the sound of running water in the bathroom, and wondering what he had meant about

Pilar. Was it possible that this Miguel was the man she had fallen in love with and been forbidden to associate with? If it was true, then some of her bitterness at least was understandable. She remembered what Luis had said about Pilar's wish to go to university. Perhaps he had feared she might be drawn into the radical elements there too. It wouldn't be easy, but she was going to try and be nicer to Pilar, she resolved.

She realised the sound of the shower had stopped, and, turning her head, realised Luis had come back into the bedroom. His sole concession to modesty a towel draped round his hips, he was pouring himself another glass of wine. Nicola watched him, feeling suddenly uneasy as he strolled back across the room and stood beside the bed, looking down at her.

The robe she was wearing was not transparent like her nightdress, but it clung revealingly, and she regretted bitterly that she was lying on top of the bed instead of seeking the concealment of the coverlet.

Luis lifted the glass to her in a mocking toast, drank some of the wine, then set the glass down very slowly and deliberately, his eyes never leaving hers. Then he sat down on the bed beside her, leaning over her and resting his hands on the bed on each side of her body so that she was virtually imprisoned.

She said helplessly, 'You—promised . . .'

'I promised I wouldn't force you,' he said softly. 'I said nothing about a little gentle persuasion.' He bent and kissed her throat, his mouth finding its unerring way to the erratic pulse there. When he lifted his head, there were little devils dancing at the back of his eyes. He murmured, 'You're trembling, *mi amada*. Is it just panic, or could there be another reason? I think—I really think I shall have to find out.'

His mouth caressed hers warmly and sensuously, without haste or urgency, then moved lower, pushing the impeding robe aside as his tongue explored the hollow at the base of her throat. He lowered his whole weight on to the bed, and slid his hand into the neckline of the robe, his thumb stroking softly along her shoulder.

His lips followed the same caressing path, and his hand moved downwards, cupping her rounded breast in his palm while his fingers stroked gently across her swollen nipple.

Nicola stifled a gasp, and her body tensed.

'Relax, *mi querida*,' Luis said huskily against her skin. 'I am not going to hurt you, or make demands of you. I just want to share a little pleasure with you . . .'

A little pleasure. His words seemed to quiver along her nerve-endings. She was half mad for him already. It was torture to deny the response she yearned to give. It was misery to lie unyielding, when what she wanted was to twine herself around him, giving him kiss for kiss and so much more.

He was kissing her breasts now, his mouth touching the soft flesh with lazy sensuality, the flicker of his tongue re-creating the pleasure his questing fingers had begun.

Nicola thought desperately, 'I have to stop him—now, or it will be too late.'

His wickedly experienced hands were travelling again, stroking down her body in total mastery, and she said hoarsely, 'Luis—please . . .'

His mouth smiled against her body. 'Willingly, *amada*. Anything you desire.' His hand slid from her hip down the smooth curved length of her thigh, and back, easing aside the folds of her robe as he did so.

The breath caught in her throat. 'You mustn't . . .'

'I must,' he contradicted softly. 'Ah, *querida*, you know that I must . . .'

Her eyes widened endlessly, looking up into his. The caressing, exploring hands were opening up new dimensions of sensation she had never dreamed existed, and she heard herself groan softly.

The dark eyes were intensely brilliant as they watched

her. He whispered, 'Do I please you, *querida*? Tell me that I do.'

There was an odd note in his voice. Something like diffidence, the corner of her mind that was still working, registered incredulously, as if he was some callow boy with his first love instead—instead of a practised seducer for whom a woman's body and a woman's responses held few mysteries.

And for a moment she saw Carlota Garcia so clearly that she might actually have been physically present in the warm shaded room, the serenely beautiful face contorted with passionate pleasure as she responded totally to the same caresses, from the same man.

She heard herself moan, 'No—oh, no . . .' and then she twisted away from him, striking his hands away from her body, levering herself desperately across the bed and burying her flushed unhappy face in the pillow.

Luis said her name on a shaken breath, and his hands came down on her shoulders to lift her back into his embrace, and she almost wailed, 'Don't touch me! I—I can't bear it!'

There was a long silence, then he said, 'What hypocrisy is this? You want me, or did you imagine that I would not know?'

'Oh, yes,' she said dully, still keeping her face averted. 'But I expect you could make a stone statue want you. God knows you've had enough experience.'

'Jealous, *mi amada*?' He actually sounded amused.

'No,' she said. 'Just—not interested. How could I be when—when I already love someone?'

'Indeed?' he drawled, the grip on her shoulders tightening painfully. 'And who is he?'

She said, 'I'll make a bargain with you, *señor*. I won't enquire too closely into your private life, and you can leave me mine.'

The cruel grip fell away from her shoulders. She lay very still and heard him leave the bed, the rustle of his clothes as he dressed, and then the slam of the door.

She was alone, which was what she had aimed for, but it was a sterile victory, because it had left her lonely also, and afraid.

There was a nightmare quality about the days which followed. The guests departed, and Nicola found herself living at the *hacienda* in the old hostile atmosphere. Only Luis was no longer her shield against it. For one thing, he was rarely there, at least during the daytime. When he was around, he treated her civilly when other people were present, and as if she did not exist when they were alone.

She had not expected he would return to her room, but he slept there each night he was at the *hacienda*. Or she supposed he slept. His breathing was even, and he never moved, or spoke to her or touched her. Nicola herself found sleep elusive, and when it came it brought wild disturbing dreams, so that she often awoke with tears on her face. And one recurring dream was the worst of all.

It seemed to happen on the nights when Luis was away, and it always began in the same way, with her riding in Luis' arms on Malagueno, safe and warm and secure, the queen of the world. It was so real that she could feel the warmth of his body, the brush of his lips on her hair, but as she turned to smile at him, to offer him her lips, everything changed. The face under the wide-brimmed hat was blank, without recognisable features, and the arms which held her were a choking prison. She usually woke up at this point gasping for breath, but then one night the dream went on and the face of the man who held her began to take shape, and with a cry of protest she realised it was Ewan, smiling triumphantly at her. Still protesting, she began to struggle against him, but his hold was too strong, he was shaking her, and she moaned his name, turning her head wildly from side to side in rejection.

Then, suddenly, her eyes snapped open and she saw

the shimmering wings of the butterfly spread like a
beneficent canopy above her. And she saw too that Luis
was there, leaning over her, holding her wrists, his
shoulders and chest bronze in the lamplight. For a
moment she thought she was dreaming still. He had not
been expected back that night, and she had fallen asleep
alone in the big bed.

She said with a little gasp, 'I was dreaming.'

'Not for the first time.' He released her wrists, and
moved away from her. Nicola wanted to say, 'Don't
leave me. Please hold me,' because she was still shaking,
but it was already too late. He pushed the covers aside
and got out of bed, standing naked for a moment while
he retrieved his robe.

He said, 'I'll ring for Maria. She can make you a
tisana to calm you. And I will spend the rest of the
night in my own room.'

Nicola watched helplessly as the door closed behind
him. There was a kind of finality about it, as if he had
decided that it was time to put an end to this pretence
of normality about their marriage.

She didn't want the *tisana* which Maria brought her,
but she drank it anyway, and whatever it contained
worked like a charm, because when she eventually
opened her eyes, it was almost the middle of the day.

She dressed hurriedly and went downstairs, to find a
furious row raging. Luis, it seemed, had gone early into
Santo Tomás, returned sooner than expected and
summoned Pilar to the study where they could be heard
shouting at each other. As Nicola hesitated in the hall,
wondering rather helplessly whether she should intervene, and what on earth she could say or do if she did,
the study door opened and Pilar erupted like a small
fury, and ran up the stairs, clearly in floods of tears.

She did not appear at the midday meal, or at dinner
that evening, and Luis, in a fouler mood than Nicola
had ever seen him, would have gratified his family by
absenting himself as well. After he had systematically

bitten everyone's head off in turn, Dona Isabella rose to her feet, quivering with outrage, and announced majestically that she was withdrawing to the *salón* as her appetite had been destroyed by her nephew's lack of consideration.

'I regret that married life has not improved your temper,' she added acidly, giving Nicola a scathing look as she swept from the room.

Nicola stared down at her half-finished plate, her face burning. As she looked up, she encountered a look of commiseration from Ramón, and she gave him a wavering smile in return.

'Perhaps you would prefer to be alone together,' Luis said silkily from the head of the table. 'Do not hesitate to tell me if you find my presence an inhibition.' His eyes glittered dangerously as he stared at them.

Ramón cast his eyes to the ceiling, pushed back his chair, and left the room in silence, leaving husband and wife confronting each other from either end of the long and shining table.

Nicola thought it would be pleasant to pick up every plate, glass and piece of cutlery on the table and throw them at Luis' head, screaming very loudly all the while, but she decided that the soft answer which was supposed to turn away wrath might be a better bet in the circumstances.

She said, 'I don't know what Pilar has done to anger you, Luis, but if I can help in any way . . .'

'So you actually wish to be of some use, do you?' he said harshly. 'Perhaps if you had taken the trouble to be friendly to Pilar, to attempt to win her over and be a companion to her, then this whole situation might have been avoided.'

The injustice of it made her blink. Over the past miserable three weeks she had done everything possible to try and win Pilar over, but the girl's hostility to her was inexorable. She spent long hours in her room, reading parcels of books sent to her from Mexico City.

Nicola would have liked to have borrowed some of them, but a tentative suggestion had resulted in such a chilly negative that she had never dared ask again.

She had asked Pilar more than once if they couldn't ride together, but had met with a curt refusal. And she knew perfectly well that Pilar had scorned Luis' direct orders, and invariably rode out alone, being missing sometimes for several hours. And yet the only time Nicola had tried to escape on her own from the atmosphere at the *hacienda*, she had encountered Ramón, who had spoken to her quite severely about taking unnecessary risks before he escorted her back to the stables, and to the unspoken but no less potent criticism of Juan Hernandez. Perhaps that was why Pilar got away with her solitary rides so easily, she thought wearily. Juan Hernandez was far too busy keeping an eye on her to perform the same service for his master's young cousin.

'Pilar hates me,' she protested. 'I have tried. Really I have . . .'

'Of course you have, *amiga*,' Luis interrupted derisively. 'No half measures in your efforts to achieve harmony with us all. Who should know that better than myself?'

Her lip trembled. 'That isn't fair! I—I didn't ask you to leave my room last night.'

'No, that was a decision I managed to make for myself,' he said grimly. 'And you should be grateful for it, *querida*, because if and when I return to your bed it will be to end this—half-marriage of ours, whether you are willing or not.'

She said faintly, 'I don't understand.'

'No? Then allow me to explain, my charming, chaste little fraud. I have no wish to lie beside you night after night, suffering the agonies of the damned, only to hear you call out another man's name in your dreams.' She gasped, and he said, 'Exactly, *amiga*. Next time you speak a man's name in my bed, it will be my name, and in circumstances I leave to your imagination.'

She began, 'But, Luis . . .'

'Oh, I am sure you have some perfectly reasonable explanation, my lovely cheat. Who is this—Ewan? The great passionate love you once mentioned to me—the one that still holds your heart?'

'It isn't as you think——' Nicola began desperately, trying to push out of her mind that it was exactly what she had intended him to think.

'But then what is? Meanwhile, *querida*, here is a thought for you to take upstairs with you. One of these nights I shall come to you, and I swear that this time no—simulated terror, no cowering in corners, no dreams of other men are going to hold me away.' He pushed his chair back and left the room.

Nicola leaned limply back in her chair. Unwillingly her eyes lifted to meet the painted gaze of Doña Manuela, which seemed in her imagination to twinkle with amused sympathy.

'It was all right for you,' Nicola addressed the long-deceased beauty in her thoughts. 'Your husband loved you so much that he carved out his own empire for you to rule over.' Her glance went to the red rose Doña Manuela held in her hand, and she sighed. 'And when he gave you that, he probably meant every petal of it.'

She prepared for bed that night feeling miserably apprehensive, aware that Maria was sending her puzzled glances. She lay awake half the night, waiting for the door to open, but Luis did not appear, and she didn't know whether to be glad or sorry.

But when she went down to breakfast the following day and heard that he had left for Sonora and would probably be away for several days, she knew that she was sorry.

Doña Isabella was at breakfast, heaving martyred sighs, but Pilar was not, and when she had finished her meal, Nicola decided to take her courage in both hands and seek the girl out.

It was with something of an effort that she knocked on her bedroom door. After a short pause, the door was flung open and Pilar confronted her.

Nicola smiled, feeling awkward. 'I wondered if you would care to go riding with me today.'

'No, I should not.' Pilar's eyes flashed. 'Has Luis set you to spy on me?'

'No, of course not. Why should he?' Nicola suppressed a sigh. 'It's just that—I think he would like us to be—better friends.'

Pilar gave her a contemptuous look. 'I do not wish to be your friend. Have I not made it plain? I do not need your company—or your patronage, Señora de Montalba,' she added with heavy irony. 'Who are you to marry into our family? A nobody without background or breeding. An *Inglesa*, with hair like straw—thin, without breasts or hips. A girl whom my cousin saw and fell in love with. *Dios*, he must have been mad! But his madness has not lasted. The whole world knows he has tired of you, and no longer sleeps in your bed.'

Nicola could not restrain her indrawn breath. But what else could she have expected? she thought miserably. In a small enclosed society like this, everyone's actions were under a microscope.

She tried again. 'Pilar, when people are unhappy they often say and do things they don't mean, so I'm going to pretend you didn't say that. I want to help—really I do.'

'Then help yourself, *señora*,' Pilar said maliciously. 'What a fool you are! Why did Luis have to marry you? Why did he not just keep you in an apartment in Monterrey as he has his other women?' She giggled suddenly. 'And today he has not gone to Sonora alone. Carlota Garcia has gone with him. I heard him arrange it yesterday, so . . .'

Nicola lifted her hand and quite deliberately slapped Pilar's cheek hard.

'*Puta!*' The Mexican girl's eyes blazed at her. 'I will

make you sorry that you were ever born!' She slammed the heavy door in Nicola's face.

Nicola stepped back involuntarily, and collided with Ramón, who was just emerging from his own room on the other side of the corridor.

'What has happened?' He sounded alarmed as he steadied her.

'A little feminine squabble,' Nicola said slowly and evenly.

Ramón groaned. 'Is she still jealous of you? The good God only knows why she should be. She never wanted Luis until Madrecita put it into her head that she should—but I suppose her disappointment over Miguel . . .' He shrugged.

'Luis mentioned that to me once,' Nicola said slowly. 'At least, he didn't tell me the man's name, but I guessed.'

Ramón grimaced. 'It is not hard to guess. In many ways they were well matched. Miguel is a firebrand and Pilar was swept off her feet by him. There was no reason why she should not be. He and Luis had attended university together, and been friends since childhood. He was a constant visitor here, so it was a tragedy when his political activities led him into trouble with the authorities.' He sighed again. 'He had a good law practice too, until he decided it was more moral to become a *peon*. He was given a small grant of our land, and built a cabin there, but he did not work the land—it was harder labour than he had imagined, I think—and even the cabin is now derelict.'

'Not quite derelict,' said Nicola, flushing slightly as he gave her a questioning look. 'Luis and I once—spent the night there.'

'So that was where.' Ramón digested this for a moment or two. 'Obviously we knew that you had been somewhere together, but Luis said nothing—and one does not ask him what he does not volunteer.'

She said in a low voice, 'Ramón, what did he tell

your mother about how—we met? Can you remember?'

He groaned. 'Can I ever forget? Madrecita was in a fury, swearing that Luis insulted her by installing one of his—ladies under her roof, and Luis gave her one of his cold looks and said that you were his future wife. Madrecita screamed and said, "A stranger—a creature you have only just met!" And Luis said, "I fell in love with her the moment I saw her." '

Nicola was silent, remembering how she had asked Luis what story he had told them, and he had said, *'Not the truth, but a story to fit . . .'*

Ramón glanced at her. 'You are very pale, Nicola. What is it? Not this silly quarrel with Pilar?'

It was hardly that, Nicola thought. There had been an almost frightening venom in the other girl.

'Perhaps,' she said. She forced a smile. 'I need some air, I'll go for a ride, I think.'

'But not alone,' he said anxiously. 'Do not even attempt it. There are all kinds of rumours, and Luis has ordered constant patrols.' He paused. 'It is why he was so angry with Pilar. Miguel Jurado is said to be somewhere in the locality again. One of the *peons* was bribed to bring Pilar a note asking her to meet him in Santo Tomás, only the man brought it to Luis instead. As she has been forbidden to have any communication with Miguel, you can understand why Luis reacted as he did.'

And she could also understand Pilar's reactions, Nicola thought a little sadly as she made her way to her room to change into her jeans and boots. She had insisted on wearing the close-fitting denims she would have worn in England for riding, and several pairs had been brought from Santo Tomás for her, even though Doña Isabella heartily disapproved of the way in which they outlined her slim hips and legs. The older woman considered a divided skirt more suitable attire for the wife of Don Luis.

When she had changed, and picked up her hat and

gloves, Nicola paused for a moment, looking at herself in the mirror. Pilar had a point, she conceded reluctantly. She had no reason to intervene in anyone else's personal affairs when her own were in such a mess.

As it was, her unthinking attempt to salvage some dregs of self-respect had simply exposed her to a bitter reckoning that could happen at any time.

And the bitterest part of all was that even if she were to tell Luis the whole truth—that she loved him to the point of despair—he would not believe her.

CHAPTER EIGHT

NICOLA sat with her back against a sun-drenched rock, wondering what to do for the best. Three days had passed since her quarrel with Pilar and relations between them hadn't improved one iota since then, she thought ruefully. Luis was expected back the following day, and he was sure to sense the atmosphere, and would probably blame her, which would make their reunion even less joyous than it already promised to be.

She made a little sound halfway between a sigh and a groan. Was she the only one at the *hacienda* who saw what was going on, and drew conclusions from it? Ramón, of course, was too busy, leaving the *hacienda* after an early breakfast, and often not returning until late in the day. But didn't Doña Isabella ever wonder where her daughter got to?

Each day since Luis' departure, Pilar had taken her horse and vanished for several hours at a time. Nicola had tried to follow more than once, but each time she had lost the trail, even though she suspected she now knew where Pilar headed each time.

Nor had it been easy, getting rid of her own assiduous escort, but she had managed it by saying mendaciously that she was going to meet Don Ramón. There had been some raised eyebrows and subdued mutterings in the stables, but she had been allowed to take Estrella and ride off unhindered. What would happen if Juan Hernandez ever checked out her story with Ramón, she chose not to think about.

She supposed she was a fool even to consider trying to help Pilar after everything that had passed between them, but she was doing it for Luis' sake, she thought, and that changed everything. He would be angry if he ever thought she had stood idly by and watched his young cousin ruin her life, as she seemed likely to do.

Nicola had little doubt that Pilar went every day to meet Miguel Jurado, and that although the letter Luis had intercepted had mentioned Santo Tomás as a rendezvous, they actually met at the *ejido*. That was the direction Pilar had taken each day, even though she had always slightly varied her route. Nicola knew this because she had taken the trouble to check a map of the estate which was kept in Ramón's office, but she had never dared ride that far herself.

She had wanted to several times, but on each occasion in the past something had held her back, reminding her how many memories that she might now find painful were attached to the place.

Nevertheless today she was quite determined. She was going to ride to the *ejido* and confront Pilar, and Miguel Jurado, if necessary. She was going to try and convince the girl that there was no future with a man who was having to live virtually in hiding, but if she failed—if Pilar refused to listen, as was more than likely, then she would just have to tell Luis the whole messy story when he returned from Sonora. That was something she could use to make Pilar see sense, she thought. The girl might rail against his autocracy, but she seemed to have a real respect for his anger.

She had not attempted to follow Pilar this time. She had ridden out ahead of her, and was waiting in the shelter of some rocks until Pilar could reasonably be expected to have arrived at the *ejido*.

She got up, dusting off her jeans, and whistled to Estrella, who came to her side stepping daintily. Nicola caressed the soft nose. The relationship between horse and rider could be such a simple one, she thought, with trust and affection on both sides.

Her solitary rides had given her plenty of time to think about Luis and herself, and she knew now she had been all kinds of a fool to allow pride to get in her way. All she had achieved was to turn him back to Carlota Garcia. He was not a man to accept kindly a period of enforced celibacy when solace in his mistress's arms was only a comparatively short distance away.

And I, Nicola thought savagely, gave him up to her without even a struggle. I could have fought. I've novelty value for him, at least, and I'm younger than she is. And I can give him the child he wants. All I have to do is accept this marriage on his terms—go to him, tell him that I want him.

She sighed. Perhaps if they were close physically, then the emotional and spiritual rapport she craved might follow—one day.

Even though she had carefully checked out the route, it was further than she thought to the *ejido*, and she realised that she was not going to make it back to the *hacienda* for the midday meal. She moved her shoulders wearily. Well, probably she would not be greatly missed.

She reined in Estrella and looked down the slope at the small building, her eyes narrowing as she realised there was a wisp of smoke coming from the chimney. Either the authorities were incredibly obtuse, or Pilar and Miguel were suffering from an overdose of bravado, she thought.

She approached with caution, even though she couldn't see Pilar's horse tethered anywhere, or any other form of transport nearby either. She dismounted, and hung Estrella's reins over a convenient rail. Her boots clattered sharply on the rickety wooden verandah, but she could hear no sounds of movement or alarm inside the cabin itself, even when she knocked sharply at the door. There was no reply, so she pushed it open and went inside.

There were obvious signs that someone was in residence. The fire was lit, and the cooking pot hung over the modest flame, emitting steam and a savoury aroma which made Nicola's nose wrinkle appreciatively, reminding her how long it was since she had eaten her sweet rolls and coffee at breakfast.

The place was cleaner too, she thought incredulously. The floor had been swept, and the table scrubbed. She noticed crockery—even a bottle of wine—and the bed made up with pillows and blankets. Every modern convenience, she thought bleakly. Two glasses for the wine. Two pillows on the bed.

Oh, Pilar! What is your mother going to say about all this? she wondered silently.

The food, all the preparations seemed to suggest that Pilar and her lover would be using the cabin in the very near future. Well, she would stable Estrella in the ramshackle building at the rear and await their arrival.

She took off her hat and pitched it on to the bed, then sat down on one of the stools. The air in the cabin was warm and close, and she unfastened a couple of buttons on her shirt, fanning herself languidly with her gloves.

Just how long had this been going on? she asked herself, gazing curiously around her. She couldn't imagine Pilar working to clean up the cabin, but perhaps she had enjoyed playing house there. Nicola found it sad.

She looked at her watch, noting resignedly that it was now well past the lunch hour, and hoping no hue and cry had been started.

She got up, gave the food on the fire a quick stir to ensure that it wasn't sticking, then poured herself a glass of the wine.

'Salud,' she thought. 'To absent friends.'

All the same, she hoped they wouldn't be absent for much longer. The wine was pleasant, but it made the cabin seem warmer than ever, and after a few minutes she put her folded arms on the table and rested her head on them. She wouldn't go to sleep, she assured herself, although she could not deny she was drowsy. But she could close her eyes for a few moments. That would do no harm, because she would be sure to hear them when they arrived.

Eventually she sat up with a start, feeling slightly dazed. She had no idea what had roused her, but it certainly wasn't anyone's arrival. She was still alone, and the fire was nearly out.

Nicola got up, stretching cramped limbs. She would find some more wood, and see to poor Estrella, she thought guiltily. She opened the cabin door and went out on to the verandah, but there was no greeting whinny. The mare had gone.

For a moment Nicola stood motionless, telling herself that she was hallucinating, the result of her long ride in the sun. Then she whistled long and frantically, but without the slightest effect. She stared at the verandah rail where she had tied the mare, trying to collect her thoughts. The rail was still intact, so Estrella hadn't dragged herself free, which meant that somone had quite deliberately released her.

Pilar, she thought helplessly. Who else? She turned and went slowly back into the cabin. Could it be that all the time she had thought she was trailing Pilar, the other girl had been following her, just waiting for an opportunity to leave her stranded? After all, she had warned Nicola she would make her sorry, and Nicola supposed that Pilar had known perfectly well that she had been on her track for the last few days and had decided to teach her a lesson.

She groaned, although she supposed she should be thankful she hadn't fallen asleep earlier under her rock, otherwise Pilar might have taken the mare then, and she would be out in the open without food or water in the full heat of the day. As it was, if she had to be abandoned somewhere, at least here there was a modicum of comfort, she thought resignedly. It could have been so much worse.

But she was anxious about Estrella. Pilar could not take her back to her stable without giving herself away, and she hoped desperately that she wouldn't just turn the mare loose and leave her to fend for herself.

I'll be all right, she thought. Sooner or later someone will come looking for me, and if I'm careful with the food there should be enough for several days.

But surely even Pilar would not be that vindictive, she hoped without too much conviction. What did she hope to gain anyway, when she knew Nicola would be found eventually, and that there'd be hell to pay when she was? Yes, Luis would be angry when he found Nicola had disobeyed him by riding alone, even with the best of motives, but was that enough for Pilar? She couldn't believe it. The malice in Pilar's face that time had indicated a wish for revenge altogether deeper and darker than this rather childish trick.

The time dragged past. She was really hungry now, so she ate a little of the stew from the pot, and drank some more wine, thinking enviously of the cool dim *comedor* at the *hacienda*. Pilar would be at home by now, sitting with an innocent face, while the others wondered where she was, no doubt.

The room became hotter, and hotter. It was getting late now, she saw by her watch, and time for *siesta*, although she was too angry to be tired. But she had nothing else to do, so she took off her boots and lay down on the bed on top of the blankets, remembering the last time she had lain there with Luis' arm around her, holding her close to the curve of his body. She sighed, twisting restlessly on the pillow. So much for honour, she thought bitterly. If he had taken her that night, she would now be his slave, and she would have been saved an incredible amount of heartache, even if it was at the expense of her pride.

But pride didn't seem important when you were jealous and lonely, and when you woke each night with your body crying out for fulfilment.

At last she managed to doze again for a while, and woke to find it was sunset. If she wasn't careful, it would be dark soon, and she needed to light the lamp and light the fire again. She sat up wearily, swinging her legs to the floor, then tensed as she thought she heard the sound of a horse's hooves. Imagination, she decided, as it had been all those other times she had heard the same thing during that interminable afternoon. And yet . . .

She bent her head, listening intently, her heart leaping with sudden hope. It was a horse. Someone was coming. Perhaps it was even Pilar who had relented and was bringing back Estrella. Maybe she wanted to do a deal for Nicola's silence about the Jurado man. She jumped up and took two quick steps towards the door.

It swung open with a crash, and Luis strode in.

Nicola halted, staring at him dazedly. He was the last person she had expected to see. He hadn't been expected before tomorrow at the earliest.

She said falteringly, noting how grim he looked, 'Luis? Did she tell you where I was? Please don't be angry. It—it was only a prank . . .'

'Yes,' he said softly, 'she told me. As to my anger, and whether or not this is a—prank, as you call it— well, I make no guarantees. Naturally you are surprised to see me.'

Nicola began, 'Well, yes . . ,' but before she could say anything else, he had cut across her.

'No doubt you are also disappointed. You have had a long and tedious wait—and all for nothing. You must be asking yourself even now why I am here, and not Ramón, and I must tell you, *chica*, that my cousin has had the good fortune to sustain a broken collarbone, so he will not be able to join you. A fall from his horse this morning,' he added sardonically.

'Join me?' All her initial joy at seeing him was subsiding under the growing conviction that something was terribly wrong. 'I don't understand.'

'Neither did I—at first. I concluded my business in Sonora sooner than I had anticipated, so I came back to the *hacienda*—to see you, *amiga*, to try and put things right between us—isn't that amusing? I found the place in confusion. Ramón had had this accident, and the doctor had been sent for. Then one of the servants asked to speak to me. Earlier, before Ramón was brought home, she had cleaned his room, and found this——' He extended his hand. The butterfly clip he had given her lay in his palm.

'But—but that's impossible!' Her brain was reeling. She hadn't worn the clip since their wedding night. She had put it away in the case with the rest of the jewellery he had given her.

'Is it, *querida*?' That dreadful quietness in his voice, and the setting sun filling the room with the colour of blood. 'I asked her where she had found it, and eventually, reluctantly she told me. In the bed of Señor Don Ramón.' He spoke these last words with a cold terrible precision.

Nicola said, 'She's lying.'

'She is a good, honest woman, who has served our family for many years. As she gave me this—thing——' he tossed it to the floor at Nicola's feet '—there were tears in her eyes.'

She said desperately, 'Luis, I swear to you that if this woman found my clip where she says she did, I don't know how it got there.'

'Don't you, my beautiful wife? Then you lack imagination, because a very obvious explanation occurs to me. But then you have so many other virtues, don't you—the domestic ones, for example. You have taken a miserable hovel and turned it into a love nest. I congratulate you.'

She exclaimed with a gasp, 'You can't think that I did all this! This was how it was when I arrived—the food, the wine—everything. I was looking for Pilar.'

'An amazing coincidence, *chica*, because she was also looking for you, but a long way from here. She found your horse wandering loose near the *hacienda* and took charge of her, afraid that something might have happened to you. Juan Hernandez and some of the men searched the immediate vicinity in case you had suffered the same fate as Ramón, but when there was no sign of you, Pilar confessed she might know where you had gone.'

The red sun was slipping away now below the horizon, and a web of darkness was slowly spinning round her.

'She told me she had kept silent before only because of her love for her brother, but that she had known for some time that you were meeting secretly here at the cabin. That she had heard him mention the place to you one morning—outside his bedroom,' he added silkily. 'Do you deny it?'

'Not the last bit, no, but we were talking about your friend Miguel Jurado—about the possibility that he might be seeing Pilar. Ask Ramón if you don't believe me.'

'I do not believe you,' he said. 'As for asking Ramón, the doctor has given him something to make him sleep. I said, did I not, that he was fortunate to break his collarbone, because if he had not, *querida*, I would most assuredly have broken his neck.'

There was a savagery in his voice which terrified her. She said, almost weeping, 'Luis—please—you can't believe all those lies! Pilar hates me, you know that. She would say anything . . .'

'That I considered.' His voice was meditative. 'Yet Juan Hernandez has no reason to hate you, and he told me in all innocence that several times this week you had left the *hacienda* alone, saying you were to meet Ramón.'

'Oh God—yes, I've said that, but it was just an excuse I invented, so that I could be alone.'

'Alone with your lover. So eager to be alone with him, *chica*, that you could not even tie up a valuable horse properly.' Luis began to take off his gloves, very slowly. 'Ramón must have succeeded most admirably with you. The next hour should prove—instructive.'

'What do you mean?' Nicola asked hoarsely.

He shrugged. 'Because an accident has robbed you of your lover, you need not be totally deprived of entertainment, *amada*. I've never followed in Ramón's footsteps before, so it will be interesting to learn what you've discovered in his arms about pleasing a man.'

She began to back away, but he followed her until the table blocked off any further retreat.

Her voice was desperate. 'Luis! I swear to you that Ramón isn't my lover. The only time I've been in his arms was at the wedding . . .' Her voice trailed away as she realised that it had probably been a mistake to remind him.

He said, 'I remember that only too well. Do you think I haven't seen you together—seen the way you look at him—smile at him, you bitch, as you've never smiled at me.' He took a handful of her hair, and jerked her head back, forcing her to meet his gaze. 'Smile at me now, *mi corazón*, and I may take the trouble to please you as well as myself when the time comes.'

His grip on her hair hurt, and she moaned in pain as well as fear as she begged, 'Luis—no—please . . .'

His fingers insolently probed her unfastened shirt, seeking the swell of her breast, then slid down to the waistband of her jeans, tugging at the zip. She began to struggle, and he bent his head and kissed her on the mouth. It was a hard bruising kiss, which held neither tenderness nor very much desire. It was merely an effective means of silencing further protest while he achieved his objective.

He picked her up, and dropped her on to the bed, joining her there immediately, almost casually unfastening his own clothes as he did so.

'Oh God—no!' Her voice broke. 'Not like this—please! Not like this.'

'You find my attentions lack finesse, *señora*? Luis asked with savage mockery. 'When you deny a starving man food, you must expect him to snatch at crumbs.'

His mouth burned on her uncovered breasts, and fear and misery notwithstanding, she felt her body shiver with pleasure. In spite of everything, he was who he was, and her starved senses knew it, and hungered in their turn.

'Show me what he has taught you.' His voice was relentless. His hands moved on her mercilessly, exploring every inch. 'Does he do this to you—and this?'

'No,' she moaned. The excitement he was engendering in her was almost intolerable in spite of his cruelty, and her body twisted restlessly against his, arching involuntarily to meet him when the moment came.

She was transfixed by pain. She had never dreamed anything could hurt so much, and a brief cry escaped her before she sank her teeth into the softness of her inner lip so deeply that she could taste blood in her mouth. Her whole body tautened instinctively, rejecting the starkness of the invasion she had been subjected to, and a tear escaped her closed lids and trickled scaldingly down the curve of her cheek.

Above her Luis was suddenly motionless, and she could only be thankful, because if he moved, if he sought to further his possession of her, she thought she might faint.

She felt his hands cup her face, smoothing back the dishevelled hair, and her eyes opened slowly and unwillingly. His face was only inches from hers, and in spite of the dim light in the cabin, she could see the horrified comprehension dawning in his eyes. Then with a long shaken groan, he rolled away from her, and lay with one arm flung across his face.

Nicola lay trembling, waiting for the ache in her body to subside. At last she sat up slowly, pulling the edges of her shirt across her breasts, and looking to see where the rest of her clothing lay tumbled on the floor where he had thrown it.

Luis said, 'Be still,' in a voice she barely recognised.

He lifted himself off the bed, re-fastening his own clothes with swift jerky movements. Then he fetched her clothes and brought them back to the bed. She put out a hand to take them from him, but he ignored it completely, dressing her as gently as if she had been a child. He fetched her discarded boots and fitted them on her feet, then wrapped her carefully in the blanket they had been lying on before he lifted her in his arms and carried her to the door.

Outside, the dark shape that was Malagueno lifted his head and whinnied softly.

Luis paused suddenly and looked down at her. He said hoarsely, '*Por Dios*, Nicola—speak to me—say something!'

She said quietly, 'Pilar told me she would make me sorry I was born. She has succeeded beyond her wildest dreams.'

Lights seemed to be blazing all round the *hacienda* as they approached. As Luis lifted her down, Nicola whispered, 'I can walk,' but again he ignored this, and carried her into the hall, which seemed to be full of people, all of them talking and exclaiming at once. Nicola turned her face into Luis's shirt, thankful for the sheltering blanket.

She heard Doña Isabella's voice, high and wailing. 'Luis, where have you been? Pilar has gone—run away—eloped with that scoundrel, that outlaw Miguel Jurado! You must follow her—you must bring her back at once. The shame—the disgrace—*ay de mi*!'

Luis paused, one foot on the bottom stair, and said something brief, succinct and obscene in Spanish. Doña Isabella gave a gasp, turned purple and sagged back against the uncertain support of her maid, a gaunt woman, while Luis continued up the stairs leaving a mystified silence behind him.

He took Nicola to her room, and put her gently down on the stool in front of her dressing table.

'Shall I fetch Maria to you?'

'No—please.' The blanket was slipping, and she could see bruises appearing on her shoulders under her loosened shirt, and knew there would be other marks on her breasts and thighs. She bruised relatively easily, and his handling of her had not been gentle.

After a brief hesitation, Luis went into the bathroom and she heard the sound of running water. She let the blanket drop to the floor with a little shudder, then stripped off the shirt. She looked into the mirror and saw that Luis had returned and was standing behind her, looking at the marks on her body with an expression of such bleak anguish that she wanted to weep—not for herself, but for him.

The bath was half full of warm scented water and she relaxed into it gratefully. Luis had not accompanied her into the bathroom. He had asked instead what she wanted him to do with the clothes and blanket she had left on the floor, and she had said, 'Get rid of them—please.'

When she got out of the bath, he reappeared and stood waiting with a towel. He enveloped her in it, then took her hand and led her back to the bedroom, and the wide bed with its turned-back covers. He lifted her into the bed, unwrapped the towel and removed it, then drew the covers up over her body. His face was taut and very contained, and there was no expression in his eyes.

He said very quietly, 'Sleep well,' and made to turn away. Nicole put out a hand and gripped his sleeve.

'Luis, stay with me, *por favor*.'

He hesitated for so long she thought for one terrible moment he was going to refuse, then he nodded curtly and sat down on the edge of the bed to remove his boots. Making no attempt to undress, he lay down beside her, but outside the covers, and his arm went round her, drawing her gently against him. She rested her head on his shoulder. There was no violence any more, she thought, no anger or fear, no high emotion,

or even particularly man and woman. Just two tired,
unhappy people drawing close for comfort.

And she thought, 'I'm safe,' before she fell asleep.

She still felt safe the next morning when she awoke,
her hand reaching to touch Luis for reassurance even
before she opened her eyes. But she was alone, and the
space beside her was empty, and she was suddenly wide
awake and sitting up in swift alarm.

Someone was watching her, and she turned and saw
Carlota Garcia sitting beside the bed, looking soignée
and beautiful in a black and white dress.

For a moment Nicola felt she must still be asleep and
having another nightmare, then she realised it was all
too real, and she dived at the covers, dragging them up
to hide herself, her cheeks suddenly crimson.

Carlota Garcia smiled, her face pleasant and friendly.
'*Buenos dias, señora.* Luis asked me to sit with you. He
did not wish you to wake alone.'

Nicola said stiffly, 'That was—considerate of him.'
She tried to anchor the slipping sheet more firmly round
her breasts.

Señora Garcia rose. 'Would you be more comfortable
in a nightgown? Tell me where they are kept and I will
fetch one for you.'

Unwillingly, Nicola directed her, and Carlota Garcia
came back with a drift of palest yellow over her arm.
She dropped it deftly over Nicola's head and turned
tactfully away while she did the rest. Nicola prayed she
would go, but instead she resumed her seat beside the
bed.

She said, 'Doña Nicola, I think someone has been
repeating ancient gossip to you. I knew at the wedding
that there was something wrong—you have honest eyes,
pequeña—so perhaps I may speak frankly to you?'

Nicola looked down at her folded hands. 'If you
wish.'

'I do wish it.' Carlota Garcia paused. 'A long time
ago, I was lonely and very miserable. My husband had

died, and I had loved him. I found that to be a widow did not stop me also being a woman. Luis had been my husband's friend, my family's friend and mine too.' She paused again. 'And for a brief time, it is true, we were more than—just friends. It was good, and I do not regret it. I said I would be frank with you. But it is over, and has been so for longer than I care to remember. I have a full and happy life again, and Luis, I hope, is still my friend, but no more than that.'

'But he still visits you, *señora*,' Nicola said in a low voice. 'Can you deny that?'

'No—but the visits he has made recently, the meetings we have attended together have had no personal motive. They have been prompted only by our mutual concern for my brother.'

'Your brother? I don't think I understand?'

Señora Garcia sighed. 'Did no one tell you, Doña Nicola, that Miguel Jurado is my brother? Luis has been using his influence to try and win him some kind of amnesty. The man he wounded has made a full recovery, praise God——' she crossed· herself —'so that the charges he may face are not so severe as they might have been.' Her eyes were full of sudden tears. 'Forgive me, but this is a great sadness to me. I always believed that Miguel would be a great man—a great lawyer, and instead he has chosen to live his life outside the law.'

'And Luis has been trying to help him?'

'Luis does not forget their past friendship, although he cannot condone what Miguel has done. And now of course he has even more reason to be angry with him.'

'Oh,' Nicola said slowly. 'Pilar.'

'*Sí*—that is why I am here.' Señora Garcia sighed again. 'They arrived at my house last night, demanding that I should help them, but of course I refused. Miguel cannot take the responsibility of a wife, with all that he has to face. I said at once that they must return here, and Pilar became very agitated, and said she would never come back. I questioned her, naturally, but it was

Miguel who finally obtained the truth from her. She admitted everything—her dislike of you, her jealousy, her wish to punish Luis, and the terrible means of revenge that she took. She knew that you suspected her, and decided to lay a trap for you at the *ejido*. She stole your butterfly and left it in Ramón's room in case anything went wrong with her original plan. She could not guess, of course, that Ramón would break his collarbone, but it was a blessing that he did so, otherwise the repercussions might have been truly dreadful.'

She leaned forward and took Nicola's hand. '*Señora*, I ask you to believe that if my brother had known anything of what she intended, he would have prevented it. He has been horrified by her conduct, but even so he does not think she is truly evil, just spoiled and misguided, and eaten with jealousy of anyone more happy than herself.'

Nicola winced inwardly. Did that really apply to her? Did she seem happy to others? Was it possible they didn't feel the inner tension in her?

She said, 'What are you suggesting, *señora*—that I should just overlook what she did?'

Carlota Garcia grimaced slightly. 'That is hardly possible. And Luis has declared that he will no longer harbour her under his roof—so I have invited her to stay with me. She can help with my correspondence and make herself useful in various ways. It will stop her thinking so much about herself, and later perhaps she can continue her education. This time, her mother's protests will go unheeded, I think.'

Nicola stared down at the butterflies on the coverlet. 'Was Luis—very angry with her?'

Señora Garcia shrugged. 'I would not have wished to face him. I do not know what he said to her, because they spoke in private, but afterwards she wept and wept. One could not see her without pitying her. And as for her mother, I do not think Doña Isabella will ever speak again,' she added with wry amusement. 'She is mortified to her soul by what Pilar has done.'

Nicola could only pity both mother and daughter. She had faced Luis' anger and contempt, and the memory hung over her like a shadow, in no way diminished by the almost austere consideration he had shown her on their return to La Mariposa. Her heart seemed to contract as she remembered it. He had performed the most intimate services for her, yet had displayed no more emotion than if she had been a—a piece of statuary he had been required to look after for a while. And this morning, she had not woken in his arms . . .

She became aware that Señora Garcia was staring at her, her face concerned and slightly questioning. She said quickly, 'Perhaps I'd better get dressed, and see what I can do to restore peace.'

'I think it would be better if you remained where you are,' Carlota Garcia smiled faintly. 'There is a truce—of sorts—and Pilar is packing the rest of her things. I will be leaving with her very soon now, and it would be kind of you, Doña Nicola, to permit her to leave without having to confront you in person.' She rose to her feet. 'And now I will go and tell Luis that you are awake.'

With another brief smile, she departed.

Nicola leaned back against her pillows, trying to assimilate everything she had been told. She should have been overjoyed by Carlota Garcia's assurances, but in the light of everything else that had happened, they seemed unimportant. The agony of jealousy she had experienced each time she had thought of them together was fading under the weight of this new uncertainty.

Her teeth worried her lower lip as she watched the door, waiting for it to open.

As he entered, she thought he looked as if he hadn't slept for a week, and an aching tenderness filled her. Last night he had comforted her, now she wanted to do the same for him—to open her arms to him, to offer her body as his pillow. As he came to stand by the bed, she looked up at him, her lips curving tentatively and shyly.

If he had returned her smile, she would have reached for him, but there was no answering warmth in his eyes or on his mouth. When he spoke, his voice was cool and formal.

'Are you well this morning? The doctor is visiting Ramón, and if you wish I can arrange for him to see you.'

Nicola flushed. 'I'm fine—really I am.'

'That is good. If you would like breakfast, Maria will bring you a tray.'

'Thank you.' Oh God, she thought wildly, what's going wrong? He was treating her as if she was a guest, a stranger under his roof, demanding the conventions of politeness.

He said, 'Later—when you have eaten—perhaps you would come to the study. There are things we must discuss.'

She said shyly, 'Can't we talk about them now?' Hold me, her heart cried out to him. Make love to me.

'I would prefer to speak to you in the study. I have people to see—calls to make—certain arrangements to finalise. I am sure you understand.'

'Arrangements about Pilar?'

'Yes.' She saw the muscle in his jaw clench. 'Among others. If you will excuse me.'

He made her a brief bow, and turned away. Nicola watched him go aware of a growing dread inside her.

She forced herself to eat some of the food which Maria brought her, then bathed and dressed with immense care, brushing a silken gloss back into her hair, banishing the pallor from her cheeks with subtly applied blusher, and accentuating the curve of her mouth with lipstick. She put on a simple dark green dress, with a skirt shaped like a bell, and a wide sash belt which drew attention to the slenderness of her waist.

She had planned to pin the silver butterfly into her hair, but remembered too late that it was still lying on the cabin floor where Luis had tossed it. Sudden tears rose in her eyes as she looked at herself in the mirror. Why had Pilar used that piece of jewellery out of all that Luis had given her? She had loved it so. But then, of course, that was precisely why it had been used, she thought bitterly. It was as if someone had deliberately destroyed a good luck talisman. And intuition was telling her that she was going to need all the luck she could get.

It took courage to go downstairs. Should she go straight to Luis' study, she wondered, or wait in the *salón* until he sent for her?

She was standing at the foot of the stairs, torn by indecision, when the loud clamorous peal of the doorbell almost made her jump out of her senses.

Carlos appeared, to answer the door, and Nicola turned towards the *salón*. If there were to be visitors, then her interview with Luis would have to be postponed, she thought with a kind of relief.

A voice, feminine and familiar, she realised with shaken disbelief, said, 'I wish to see the Señorita Nicola Tarrant. Is she here?'

It was Teresita. As Carlos stepped aside, she walked into the hall followed by Cliff. Nicola moved forward uncertainly, and Teresita ran to her, throwing her arms around her.

'Nicky—oh, Nicky, you are here! I could not believe your letter. Tell me it isn't true. Oh, Nicky—that man—what has he done to you?'

CHAPTER NINE

NICOLA returned the embrace, then looked at Carlos, who was looking frankly scandalised. She moistened her lips. 'That will be all, Carlos. Teresita, come into the *salón*. We can talk there.'

'We are not staying,' Teresita said firmly. 'We are leaving at once, and you are coming with us. This marriage must not happen. I will not allow it. The brute—the tyrant—he will not do this thing!'

Nicola saw Cliff look past her, and his face change as he dropped a warning hand on his wife's shoulder.

'Welcome to my house, Señorita Dominguez,' Luis said silkily. 'Or should I now call you by another name?'

Teresita gave him a defiant glance, and Cliff interposed hastily, 'Don Luis, you must wonder about this intrusion, but the fact is my wife had this letter from Nicky here, and it upset her so much she insisted we come here and get everything sorted out.'

'Usted es muy amable.' Luis' tone was ironic. 'Shall we go into the *salón*, and I will ask for refreshments to be brought.'

'We do not wish for refreshments,' said Teresita, but she went into the room he indicated. 'We have come for Nicky. She came here to save me, and I will not allow her to sacrifice herself in my place.'

Luis said icily, 'You are too late, *señora*. I regret to inform you that the sacrifice has already been made.'

Teresita gasped. 'Then we are too late? Nicky, you cannot be already married! It is not possible. How did he force you to do such a thing? *Madre de Dios*, I should never have allowed you to come here!'

'You can say that again,' Cliff muttered. '*Señor*, I don't

171

want to apportion blame here, but it seems we have one hell of a mess. Now, I want your assurance that you didn't use any element of coercion with Nicky here . . .'

Luis shrugged 'I can give no such assurance. I offered Nicola the choice between marriage, or dishonour and jail.'

Cliff's lips parted, then with a helpless gesture, he turned away in silence.

'*Tirano*—bully!' Teresita exclaimed. 'You should be made to suffer for the rest of your life for what you have done. Oh, my poor Nicky!'

Watching Luis, Nicola saw the firm lips tighten.

He said, 'Your "poor Nicky" is free to leave my house whenever she wishes. I regretted my conduct towards her a long time ago, and I intend to seek an annulment. Does that satisfy you?'

Nicola felt as if she had been turned to stone. She wanted to cry out, to utter some protest, but no words would come. She stared at Luis, her green eyes widening with shock and hurt, but he seemed oblivious to her gaze.

He was speaking to Cliff. 'Your arrival, *señor*, is in fact opportune. I presume you are willing to escort my— wife to wherever she wishes to go?'

'Sure—anything you say,' Cliff agreed, looking embarrassed to death. 'How—how soon can you be ready, honey?' He looked at Nicola.

She was still watching Luis and she saw the flicker of distaste that the casual endearment provoked.

She said shakily, 'Can you wait for a moment? I would like to speak to my husband in private.'

The pleading in her eyes met only coldness in his. For a moment she thought, panicking, that he was going to refuse. Then he gave a brief curt nod. She followed him out of the room, conscious that Cliff and Teresita were watching them in frank amazement. Once the door had closed behind them, she caught at his sleeve.

'Luis . . .'

'One moment.' He detached himself from her fingers. 'This hallway is hardly private. We had better go to my study.'

The shutters had been drawn and the room was dim and cool. He set a chair for her, and she sank into it, her eyes watching him with painful intensity.

She asked, 'Why are you sending me away?'

'You can ask me that after what has happened between us? This marriage I forced on you was madness, and it is time we regained our sanity before we harm each other further. Go away from here, Nicola, leave Mexico, and soon this brief time in your life will seem like a bad dream.'

'Another one.' She tried to smile, but her lips were trembling. 'Luis, you don't—you can't still think that I—that Ramón . . .'

'*Dios,* no!' She saw him flinch. 'No, every foul lie that bitch told is known to me. And besides,' his mouth twisted bitterly, 'had I not already proved your—innocence for myself? I behaved like an animal to you, treated you in a way I would not have treated a girl of the streets. The only way I can make amends is to give you your freedom.'

Freedom, she thought, when her love would be a chain to bind me to you for ever.

She tried to steady her voice, 'Then you don't want me any more?'

He turned a derisive look on her. 'Not want you, *chica*? You have a lovely face and an entrancing body. Who would not want you? But now I acknowledge it is hardly a sufficient basis for marriage.'

Nicola felt as cold as ice. She said, 'But you thought it was once.'

Luis gave a slight shrug, his face cynical. 'I thought I had explained that when we encountered each other, Nicola, I was bored with the prospect of the marriage which awaited me. For a time you were a—charming novelty, but now that time is past.'

She said almost inaudibly, 'You told—your family that you had fallen in love with me at first sight. Was it true—or was it just a story?'

He walked across the room and stood with his back to her, looking out through the shutters. He said quietly, 'It was just a story.'

Her breath escaped in a swift, painful sigh, then she stood up. He turned back, alerted by her movement. He said evenly, 'You will need money—and this.' He produced her passport from a drawer and slid it across the desk to her. 'When you have decided on a place of residence, perhaps you would let me know so that my lawyers can contact you.'

She said, 'As simple as that.' She picked up the passport and saw there was money inside it. She let it fall to the desk. 'I don't need your charity, Luis. I have friends, and I'm quite capable of earning my living, as I did before we met.'

He stiffened. 'Naturally, there will be a settlement . . .'

'Which I shall refuse.' She met his eyes steadily. 'I'll take the little I came with, and nothing else. Perhaps you would be good enough to say goodbye to Ramón for me.'

She went out of the room without a backward glance, and straight up to her bedroom. For a moment she stood there, looking around her almost wildly, as she tried to remember where Maria had put her shoulder bag. The girl had disapproved of its size and clumsiness and wanted to dispose of it altogether, but Nicola had refused, and she was thankful that she had done so. A brief search of one of the capacious cupboards revealed it, and she threw it on the bed and began packing things into it—her passport for a start, then a handful of underwear, and her cosmetics and toilet things. She would need a nightgown. She looked round for the yellow one she had worn earlier, but it had already been removed for laundering, and the first one she found in the chest of drawers was the exquisite confection Señora Mendez had created for her wedding night. She dropped it as hurriedly as if it had been one of the gowns of fable which scorched the unlucky wearer. Wherever she slept tonight, she would make do without one, and tomorrow she would borrow some cash from Teresita and do some essential shopping. She imagined they would take her to the Californian border, and if so she could make her way to Los Angeles, and find Elaine. There might even still be a job with Trans-Chem, and she would find herself somewhere to live, maybe beside the ocean. She liked the sea, although she hadn't seen that much of it in her life. Luis had a villa beside the ocean which she had never seen, and now she never would.

She stopped, closing her eyes, as pain tore through her. There was no profit in thinking of all the 'nevers' in her life, but how could she ban them from her mind? Never to touch him, never to kiss him, or feel the hard masculine weight of his body against hers again. Never to look up and meet his eyes across the dining table. Never to ride with him in the warm darkness under the stars. Never to feel his child stirring under her heart.

She stripped off the green dress, as if she was shedding a skin, and changed into the blue one she had worn when she first came here, tying her hair back at the nape of her neck with a wide navy ribbon.

Teresita and Cliff were waiting for her in the hall. Cliff's brows rose. 'Is this all you have?'

'No,' she said. 'But it's all I'm taking.'

'You really wish to leave like this?' Teresita put a hand on her arm. 'Surely he owes you something for treating you so callously . . .'

'He owes me nothing,' Nicola said steadily. 'Can you give me a moment while I say one last goodbye.' She walked into the dining room and looked up at the portrait of Doña Manuela. She looked at the rose, and the butterfly pinned into the dark hair, and let the pain have its way with her again. She thought, 'I really let the Mariposa legend get to me. I wanted to be like you. I wanted Luis to love me, as you were loved, but it was always impossible.'

A bewildered Carlos was standing outside as she emerged.

'You are going on a trip, *señora*?' He was clearly at a loss about her lack of luggage, and slightly disapproving too, as if he had a poor opinion of any young bride who went on a trip without her husband.

She nodded. 'Is—is Don Luis still in his study? I'd like another word with him.'

Carlos looked genuinely distressed. 'Ah, no, *señora*. The Señor has gone to the stables. He gave orders that Malagueno should be saddled for him. He could not have realised that you intended to depart so soon ...'

'It's all right, Carlos,' she said gently. 'I've already said *adios*. I was just being foolish.'

He said, '*Vaya con Dios, senora,* and come back to us soon.'

Nicola smiled waveringly, and went out to the waiting car.

Teresita and Cliff were more than kind, although Nicola guessed they must both be burning with questions. She sat in the back of the big car, and stared out of the window as it ate up the miles between La Mariposa and their eventual destination. She was too listless even to enquire where that might be.

At last they pulled into a small town, and Cliff stopped the car.

'Time to eat,' he announced.

Nicola would have preferred to remain in the car. The thought of food nauseated her, but she didn't want to upset Cliff and Teresita, so she accompanied them to a small restaurant in the central square, with a terrace overlooking the bustling market. A smiling girl brought them drinks, and they ordered black bean soup, flavoured with *epazote*, to be followed with strips of grilled steak topped with cheese, and served with *enchiladas*, fried beans, onions and chilies.

Nicola's mind was running in circles, but she forced herself to sip her drink.

Cliff was watching her. 'You look awful pale, honey.'

'And what wonder is that?' Teresita demanded warmly. 'How she has been made to suffer!'

Nicola shook her head. 'Whatever happened, I deserved.'

'I hear what you're saying, but it doesn't make much sense,' said Cliff. 'The guy has done you dirt, then and now. Okay, so what, you tried to pull with him was one crazy stunt, but hell, he didn't have to react as strongly as that about it. You don't practically kidnap a girl and make her marry you.'

She said wearily, 'It was an impulse.'

'He seems to have a lot of them,' Cliff muttered. 'And now he gets another impulse and decides enough is enough.'

Nicola bent her head. 'It—it was never a real marriage. There's no reason for either of us to feel tied by it.'

'And what are these impulses?' Teresita demanded. 'Don Luis does not give way to such things. Whenever I met him, he was always so correct—so aloof, never ruffled.'

'Except once,' Nicola reminded her with a faint smile. 'When he tried to give you a ride on his horse.'

'*Ay!*' Teresita clapped a hand to her head. 'I had forgotten. Oh, my poor mother, how mortified she was!'

'Look,' said Cliff, 'can we postpone the reminiscences? Nicky has a problem here. We're driving towards California, and I don't know that we should be because back there is a guy who forced her into some kind of weirdo marriage. Now, Nicky, you have every justification for hating his guts, but that doesn't mean you should let him get away with it like this.'

'I don't hate him,' Nicola said simply.

Teresita put down her glass and stared at her. 'Nicky, what are you saying? You cannot be serious!'

Nicola moved her shoulders wearily. 'I was never more serious in my life.' She smiled bitterly. 'Yes, he did pressure me into marrying him at first, but he didn't need to. I—I wanted him before I even realised who he was.'

Teresita said shakily, '*Dios*, you are in love with him. Then why did you leave with us?'

'Because he doesn't love me, and I was afraid to show him how much I cared. It was all a disaster from the start,' Nicola confessed miserably, but the actual statement of the problem made her begin to feel better. Sitting in the car, she had gone over that final scene with Luis over and over again, trying to make sense of what had happened. He had behaved as if he was indifferent to her, but surely if that was the case he could not have been so angry, so jealous over her supposed affair with Ramón. Surely his violent reaction proved that he must care?

But she wouldn't think about caring. He had admitted he still wanted her and she could have built on that, even if that was all there would ever be in any relationship between them.

'*Ay de mi!*' Teresita put her hand on her husband's arm. 'Cliff, we must return to La Mariposa at once.'

'No,' Nicola protested. 'It—it's over. I can't go back.'

'Nothing is over,' Teresita said severely. 'You told us that it was not a real marriage, so how can it be over when it has not even begun? And if you go to California, it never will, because Don Luis will never follow you there. He is too proud.'

'Here comes the soup,' Cliff put in practically. 'I'll drive anywhere I'm told, but not on an empty stomach. And whether Nicky wants to go on to California, or back to the *hacienda*, she needs to eat, or she'll fall flat at Don Luis' feet in a faint, and that's not the idea at all.'

It was a long, leisurely meal, and Nicola sat, chafing

silently as she forced herself to swallow as little food as she could get away with. It was mid-afternoon before they began the return journey, and she sat quietly wondering what to say, how to make things right between them.

It would not be easy, there was more than his pride to conquer. There was the sense of shame that his treatment of her the previous night had engendered, and her own shyness.

She sighed inwardly. It would have been so much less complicated if she had simply woken in his arms this morning. She could have turned to him then, convinced him somehow that the harshness of his initial possession of her was unimportant, and that she wanted him as passionately as he desired her. Her own woman's instincts would have carried her through, making stammered explanations unnecessary. Whereas now . . .

She stopped herself short. That was defeatism, and it had no place in her plans. She loved Luis, and she wanted him, and everything would be all right because it had to be.

Nevertheless, she still had her fingers crossed superstitiously as they turned under the high arched gate and drove up the private road beyond the *hacienda*. It was almost dark, and she didn't know whether to be glad or sorry about that.

Cliff halted the car in front of the main entrance, and she rang the bell.

Carlos' jaw dropped when he saw her. '*Ay, señora!* You have returned to us. Don Luis will be a happy man.'

'I certainly hope so,' she said with a calmness she was far from feeling. 'Will you arrange for a room to be prepared for Señor and Señora Arnold in the guest wing, Carlos? They'll be staying the night.'

'It is my pleasure, *señora*.' He was already moving to greet them, to collect their luggage.

Nicola took a deep breath and went up the stairs. She

had plenty of time to change before dinner, and if she hurried, there might be a chance to talk to Luis first. He would probably be in his own room now, and she would try to catch him before he went down to the *salón*, although she still wasn't sure exactly what she was going to say to him.

Lost in thought, she went into her room and walked across to the bed to switch on the big lamp. As the light came on, she nearly jumped out of her skin.

Luis was there, lying face downwards across the bed, his face buried in her pillow. He was fully dressed except for his boots which were lying covered in dust in the middle of the bedroom floor where he had clearly thrown them. On the chest beside the bed was a bottle and a used glass. Nicola glanced at it, grimacing at the faint reek of spirits, and her heart sank. Had he drunk himself into insensibility? But a further look at the bottle provided reassurance. It was still more than two thirds full, and she guessed that if he had intended to drink himself to sleep, he had been overtaken by sheer exhaustion first.

One arm dangled limply over the edge of the bed, and on the floor below something glittered faintly which had obviously fallen there from his relaxed fingers. Nicola bent, and picked up her silver butterfly.

She cradled it in her hand, her happiness soaring. He must have ridden all the way to the *ejido* to fetch it, and that had to be a hopeful sign, because it had no great intrinsic value for him to pursue. She touched the butterfly to her lips, then placed it on the bedside chest beside the glass.

Luis, she addressed him silently, my handsome, desirable, beloved, stubborn husband, it's time you woke up. She bent and lightly kissed the dishevelled black hair. He stirred immediately, but by the time he had lifted himself on to one elbow and was looking around him, she was several feet away, standing on the edge of the circle of lamplight, and smiling at him.

She said, *'Buenas noches, señor.'*

For a long moment, he stared at her. His face was still grim and set, but there was a new uncertainty in his eyes.

At last he said quietly, 'If I am dreaming, then I hope I never wake.'

'I'm not a dream, *señor*. I'm flesh and blood, as I shall soon prove to you.' She kicked off her sandals and pivoted slowly on one bare foot. 'See—I'm real. All of me.'

'I see,' he said drily. 'Nicola, what are you doing here? Why have you come back—and how?'

'Teresita and Cliff brought me. They're in the guest wing. And I'm here because you cheated me, Don Luis. Before you married me, you promised me passion, and you've cheated me. And today, I realised why.' Again she did that long slow pivot, allowing her skirt to swing out around her.

'And of course you are going to tell me.' His voice was even.

'Of course. You married me because you didn't want a dull, conventional marriage. But our life together just hasn't had the sort of excitement you wanted. So——' she smiled at him again —'I have decided that I shall just have to be more entertaining in future. Starting now.'

She began to unzip her dress. When it was completely unfastened, she slipped it off her shoulders and let it fall to the floor, then kicked it away. She risked a glance at him under her lashes and saw with heart-stopping satisfaction that she had his whole and undivided attention. She unhooked the waistband of her lacy underskirt and let it float away. She was by no means as confident as she hoped she appeared. In fact, she could easily have cracked apart with nervousness. She lifted her hands as if to unclip her bra, then raised them further to pull loose the ribbon confining her hair instead. She shook the long tawny strands over her shoulders, and moistening suddenly dry lips, reached once more to undo her bra.

She hadn't seen him move, but he was beside her, his hands slipping round her body, pulling her against him. His dark head bent over her in passionate acceptance of the mute invitation of her parted lips.

When at last she could speak, she said huskily, 'Señor, this is an outrage! The audience are forbidden to take part in the floorshow.'

'Is that so, *mi amada*?' His voice held an edge of laughter. 'Naturally, I know little of such things, but I always understood that the show was over—once the girl was naked.'

Nicola was going to say, 'But I'm not,' when she realised in time what those sensuously caressing hands had achieved while he was kissing her. She felt hot colour invade her face.

'Blushing, *querida*?' He touched his lips to one flushed cheek. 'I am sure no real showgirl would do so.'

'But I'm not a real showgirl,' she said in a low voice, staring as if mesmerised at his shirt buttons. 'I'm not even a real wife—but I love you, Luis, and I want you so much that if you don't take me, I think I'll break into little pieces,' she ended on a rush of words.

He slid a hand under her knees, swinging her up into his arms. 'Then I am at your service, *querida*,' he said softly. 'It would be a tragedy if harm should come to anything so exquisite——' he bent his head and kissed her body —'and so perfect through any neglect of mine.'

There was no longer any room for doubt and misunderstanding, and certainly none for fear. He kissed her as he lowered her gently on to the bed, and her arms clung round his neck as at last he made to draw away slightly.

'*Querida*, I'm not leaving you,' he whispered. 'I only want to take off my clothes and then . . .'

'I'll help you.' She knelt up on the bed, tugging at the

buttons on his shirt, the speed of her shaking fingers not matching her eagerness, so that she tore the buttons from their fastenings, and when at last there were no further barriers between them, and for the first time she felt the warmth and strength of him totally against her own skin, she gave a little sigh of sheer sensual delight.

His hands and mouth caressed her, arousing such unhurried, delicious torment that the last remnants of her self-control fled, and she clung to him mindlessly, her body moving against his in fevered excitement while she whispered his name against his skin. There were no inhibitions left in her response. She kissed him as he was kissing her, touched him as she had yearned to do, her hands sliding without reservation along the lean, graceful length of his naked body, knowing a stinging joy when her caresses made him groan with pleasure.

His patience with her was endless, his generosity infinite, and although she was prepared for more pain, there was none—only a shattering pleasure as he took her with him into a vortex of sensual satisfaction bordering on agony.

Later, lying dreamily content in his arms, she said, 'I tore your beautiful shirt.'

'I have numerous shirts, *amada*. If it is to be the prelude to this kind of paradise, then you may rip each of them to shreds with my blessing.' His hand cupped her breast, his fingertips drawing tiny erotic spirals on her skin.

Nicola giggled, brushing her lips against the bronze column of his throat. 'What would the servants say?'

'Nothing, if they know what is good for them,' he returned lazily.

'Luis, can I ask you something? You won't be angry?'

'Ask anything you wish, *mi mujer*. And I am never less likely to be angry in the whole of our lives together than at this moment.'

She said shyly, 'You said—paradise, but it can't have

been like that for you. You—you've had other women, and it was really the first time for me—so . . .'

'So it was also the first time for me. The first time with you, *querida*, my wife, the woman I love. Yes, I admit there have been other women, although I have not spent my entire life in bed,' he added wryly. 'And now I will make an even more shocking confession, my liberated English rose. I would rather have my wife a willing pupil in my arms than my match in experience.'

She gasped. 'That's a double standard!'

'I know, my beloved, and I am deeply ashamed.'

'You are a liar, *señor*.' She bit him delicately on the shoulder, then kissed him, her mouth lingering softly on his. 'Has anyone ever told you that you're beautiful?'

'No,' he said gravely. 'So—another first time for me. *Muchas gracias, mi amada.* And has anyone ever told you how sweet you are, how smooth and soft and completely desirable? And that I love you more than life itself?'

'Then why did you try to send me away?'

He sighed. 'What else could I do? I told myself I had ruined everything, destroyed for ever any chance we had of happiness together. I was so cruel to you, *amiga*, so clumsy and brutal, and my only excuse was that I was crazy with wanting you, and crazy with jealousy of poor Ramón.'

'That was my fault.'

'A little, perhaps,' he said. 'But it doesn't matter. I told myself it was impossible you could forgive me after what I had done to you, that I would always be terrified that you would look at me as you did on our wedding night—as if I was some kind of satyr. I lay here last night, holding you, and realised I could not face that again. But having tasted your sweetness, however briefly, I knew also that I could not go back to leading the separate lives we had lived up till then. So it seemed best to send you away.'

Nicola said in a low voice, 'Luis, I never thought of

you as a satyr. It was myself I was frightened of then—
and later—and all the things I knew you could make me
feel. I knew that I loved you, and I was scared to show
it in case you laughed at me.'

'Laughed?' He sounded shaken. 'Nicola, I would have
thanked God on my knees for one kind word, one look
from you. Before all this happened with Pilar, I had
already decided that I had been wrong to try and start
our life together here, although you seemed to like La
Mariposa. I thought I would take you away—on that
trip to the south you had planned before we met. It
would be our honeymoon, I told myself, and I would
do anything in the world to make you fall in love with
me, and with me alone. Then today after you had gone,
I rode out to the cabin to find the butterfly I had given
you. I stayed there for hours, remembering how we met,
torturing myself, and I knew I could not let you go.
When I came back I phoned the airline and booked
myself a ticket to England. I thought you might go home
to your family, and that if you did I would be there
waiting for you, asking you to come back to me on my
knees if necessary.'

Nicola's heart lifted. Teresita had been wrong about
his pride. He had been ready to sacrifice even that because he loved her.

'But instead I came to you,' she said. 'And you got
what you wanted.'

He grinned lazily. 'Indeed, *señora*, in innumerable
ways. Which particular one were you thinking of?'

'You once said that you wanted to hear your name
and no one else's on my lips,' she reminded him. 'Luis,
can I tell you about Ewan?'

He shrugged slightly. 'If you wish, *querida*. He is
hardly important.'

'No, but I don't wany any question marks from the
past cropping up in the future,' she said, knowing that
the shadow of Carlota Garcia no longer lay between
them. Briefly she told him of the events which had led

up to her leaving Zurich. 'Those dreams I had were really of you, only I'd had this letter which my parents sent on to me. They didn't know who it was from, and neither did I until I opened it. I read it, just before you came to my room on our wedding night—and it was then I realised that I'd hardly loved him at all. That when I measured it against what I felt for you, it barely existed.' She swallowed. 'I realised too why I'd never tried to run away again, and I was frightened.'

'So that was it,' he said softly. 'I knew there was something, although at first I decided you were merely absorbed in the music I had arranged for you.'

'And so I was. That was a lovely thought, Luis.' She paused. 'Why didn't you let those others play for us at the motel that night?'

He grimaced. 'Because I was just beginning to realise that my plans for you went further than mere seduction, *querida*. The serenaders thought we were lovers, which was what I had intended, and then it occurred to me that I wanted serenades for you on all kinds of occasions, and not just as a means to get you into my bed.' He kissed her mouth. 'I have cursed myself for my scruples since, believe me.'

'Oh, I do,' she assured him, lifting a hand to stroke his cheek. 'Luis, I still have that letter. Do you want to read it?'

'Only if that is what you want, *mi corazón*.'

She slipped out of his arms and went across to the dressing table, retrieving the crumpled ball of paper from the back of the drawer. Very much at his ease, Luis watched her return to the bed.

'How lovely you are.' His hand stroked her body, as she settled once more into the curve of his arm. 'I shall have to invent errands for you all over the room, *querida*, so I can watch you.'

She pulled a mischievous face at him. 'Read the letter, or I'll get dressed!'

He kissed her, his mouth warm and searching. 'Don't

count on that. I may never let you leave this room again.'

'Oh.' Nicola suddenly thought of something. 'But Luis, I must—we must. Teresita and Cliff. It's long past dinner time. They'll be wondering where we are and . . .'

'I think they have sufficient imagination to know where we are, *amada*. We will see them tomorrow. Now let me read this letter.'

He smoothed out the sheet of paper, and began to read, frowning. When he had finished, he said, 'Poor creature.'

'Ewan?' She threw him a startled glance.

'No, his wife, may her soul rest in peace.' He tore the letter in half and dropped the pieces on the floor. 'So that is the end of him. You have been spared much unhappiness with this man, *amada*. But as you say, no more question marks.'

'And the whole future ahead of us.' She pressed close to him, joyously aware that his caressing hand was once more causing tendrils of pleasure to curl along her nerve-endings. 'How nice that it contains tonight.'

'How nice that it contains you, love of my heart,' he said, and smiled down into her eyes. It was the look she had longed to see, and it made her catch her breath.

She said softly, 'Oh Luis—oh, Luis, I love you so. I— I can't begin to tell you . . .'

'Yes, you can, *mi querida*.' He began to kiss her, softly at first, and then with deepening passion. 'Tell me—like this . . .'

Harlequin® Plus

THE TROUBADORS OF MEXICO

Street musicians are part of the delight of any great city, and every culture has its own particular kind of troubador. In Mexico, it is the *mariachi*, a small band of three to five musicians who play *sons*—Mexican folk songs—in the streets and plazas of the sun-baked cities and towns.

The early *mariachis*, several hundred years ago, adopted European instruments, and today the members of *mariachi* bands make use of two violins; a *vihuela*, or five-string guitar; a *jarana*, or slightly larger guitar; and a *guitarrón*, a four-stringed bass guitar. Often the music is accompanied by a *zapateado*, a kind of tap dance performed by one of the musicians on a wooden board, which adds percussion to the music.

The *sons* played by the *mariachis* have their origins in folk music dating from before the time of the Spanish conquistadors. Almost all the words to *son* music are about women and love—and the lyrics are sweet, never tragic. Indeed, the word *mariachi* means "little Mary," from the Spanish saying, All women are the Virgin Mary.

The visitor to Mexico may encounter the *mariachis* while sipping a cool drink in a café on a hot afternoon or while sitting on a bench in a plaza at dusk. The wandering street musicians drift by with their haunting music that, like the deep rich perfume of the tropics, is as old as Mexico itself.

Take these 4 best-selling novels FREE

Yes! Four sophisticated, contemporary love stories by four world-famous authors of romance FREE, as your introduction to the Harlequin Presents subscription plan. Thrill to **Anne Mather**'s passionate story BORN OUT OF LOVE, set in the Caribbean....Travel to darkest Africa in **Violet Winspear**'s TIME OF THE TEMPTRESS....Let **Charlotte Lamb** take you to the fascinating world of London's Fleet Street in MAN'S WORLD....Discover beautiful Greece in **Sally Wentworth**'s moving romance SAY HELLO TO YESTERDAY.

Harlequin Presents...   The very finest in romance fiction

Join the millions of avid Harlequin readers all over the world who delight in the magic of a really exciting novel. EIGHT great NEW titles published EACH MONTH! Each month you will get to know exciting, interesting, true-to-life people . . . . You'll be swept to distant lands you've dreamed of visiting . . . . Intrigue, adventure, romance, and the destiny of many lives will thrill you through each Harlequin Presents novel.

Get all the latest books before they're sold out!
As a Harlequin subscriber you actually receive your personal copies of the latest Presents novels immediately after they come off the press, so you're sure of getting all 8 each month.

Cancel your subscription whenever you wish!
You don't have to buy any minimum number of books. Whenever you decide to stop your subscription just let us know and we'll cancel all further shipments.